First Lady

To A

Dope Boy 2

Written By:

Bridgette I'esha

Bridgette I'esha

Dedication

This book and all the rest of my books are dedicated to my beloved Angel my Grandmother Delores "Dee" Aldridge. I'm in tears as I write this. I can still see the smile on your face as you watched me receive my diploma. You were proud of me then, and I can only imagine how proud you would be to see the young woman and mother I have become today. Rest in Paradise Baby. Love you always 05/06/12 the day heaven gained an angel.

Bridgette I'esha

Follow me on:

Twitter @AuthorbridgetteIesha

Instagram: AuthorBridgetteIesha

Add me on:

Facebook

Facebook.com/BridgetteI'esha

Bridgette's Reading Lounge

Email: AuthorBridgetteIesha@gmail.com

Chapter One

Sirens could be heard taking over the silence of the normally quiet neighborhood. Big Jimmy was trying his hardest to find an escape route. Both of his sons were laid across the living room floor with gunshot wounds, but he knew if he didn't get out of there soon, then he would surely be making a trip downtown. Grabbing all the visible weapons, he made it to his truck undetected. "My boys got a strong bloodline running through their veins. They'll be just fine." Jimmy reassured himself as he pulled off headed towards Lincoln's Medical Center.

Across the street sat a mysterious person, in an unmarked car taking in the entire scene. "In due time all things will be revealed." The unknown person said as they vanished into the night.

*****

Bridgette I'esha

Beep…Beep…Beep was the only sounds that could be heard coming from Sharnese's hospital room. When she woke up, she was terrified. Sharnese had no clue where she was. Tubes had been placed in her mouth and nose so she could breathe. Bandages covered the huge gash on the side of her head. Frantically she pushed the call button on her bed for the nurse. Before she knew it, she was pulling the tubes out, trying to get out of the bed.

"Miss, I'm going to need you to relax and calm down." The curly-haired, blue-eyed nurse said as she rushed through the door.

Sharnese's monitor began to beep even louder. According to the machine, her excitement was causing her heartbeat to rise at an alarming rate. Sharnese sat there trying to piece everything together. No matter how hard she tried, she still couldn't figure out what was going on. Then it hit her. The incident of Murda getting shot played in her head.

"Murda! Where's Murda?" She screamed panicking, everything was coming back to her at once. Suddenly, she remembered firing the gun before she blacked out.

"Miss, again, please calm down before you upset yourself." The nurse was becoming irritated with the way Sharnese was

Bridgette I'esha

behaving, but Sharnese didn't care. She wasn't about to calm down until she received some sort of information.

The nurse name Kathy called the doctor over the intercom. Seconds later, Dr. Perez was in the room with her clipboard in hand ready to go over Sharnese's charts. This was one part of the job she hated. It was always hard for her to tell her patients certain news while recovering.

"Miss Jackson, take a deep breath and relax for me sweetie," Dr. Perez said in a calm, mellow tone while trying to do the breathing exercise herself.

It was something about the way the doctor spoke that made Sharnese listen. She really hadn't meant to give the nurse such a hard time, but not knowing the whereabouts of Murda was driving her insane. Despite the issues they were going through, he was her better half. Sharnese apologized to the nurse for her behavior and turned to the doctor for some answers.

"Dr. um…" She looked at the name tag on the doctor's white coat and continued. "Dr. Perez, can you please tell me if a Cortez Rodriguez is a patient in this hospital?" She closed her eyes, preparing for the worst.

Bridgette I'esha

Dr. Perez smiled. She loved seeing the love that the young couples displayed. It was something she never got the chance to experience. Her career was always her focus, so she never had time for a relationship or anything else for that matter. Work had always been the story of her life.

"Yes, he's here, but I will not answer any more of your questions until you listen to what's going on with you." The doctor said as she went over Sharnese's chart one last time.

"Okay Doc, hit me with it, I'm ready," Sharnese reassured the doctor.

"Well, for starters God was definitely watching over you two."

"So that means Cortez is alright?" She asked dying to know.

"I wasn't talking about him. I was referring to the one growing inside of your belly...Sharnese you're pregnant." Dr. Perez blurted out. The look on Sharnese's face was priceless. One would have thought she'd seen a ghost. The color on her face had vanished completely.

"You're kidding me, right?" Was all Sharnese could say. She was stuck in her own little world sure that her mind was playing tricks on her.

"I'm very much serious." Dr. Perez walked out into the hallway for a brief minute. When she returned she rolled in a cart with the Ultrasound machine on it. "Can you lay on your back for me?" Sharnese did exactly as she's told and lied flat on her back. "Alright, this may be a little cold."

Sharnese squirmed as the doctor placed the blue goo on her stomach. When she heard the heartbeat on the monitor, her heart melted. Instantly she fell in love with her unborn child, but it was still a bittersweet moment since she didn't know what was going on with Murda. *Me a mother? This doesn't even seem like it's possible.* Even after hearing it for herself, she still couldn't grasp the fact that she was expecting her first child.

"How is this possible? I mean, I know how it happens and all, but I never had any symptoms. I still got my period every month," Sharnese said questioning the doctor.

"Some women do in fact, have something like their menstrual cycle during the early stages of their pregnancy while

Bridgette I'esha

others have may experience it the entire time. Not all women have morning sickness or any other symptoms. Every woman is very different." Dr. Perez felt slightly bad for the young lady. She could only imagine what she was going through after being badly beaten, and finding out she would soon become a mother.

"So, are you going to tell me the condition of Cortez or not?" Sharnese said with much attitude. She had heard enough. At that moment, she didn't want to think about the baby. For all, she knew the father of her child was deceased and ready to be sent to someone's morgue.

"He's in room 208," Dr. Perez replied.

That was all Sharnese needed to hear as she left out of the room. It didn't take her long to find Murda's room. The sight of him all bandaged up brought tears to her eyes. She didn't even recognize the man before her. His face was swollen twice its size. Breathing tubes ran down his throat and in his nose. Sharnese was so concerned with Murda that she never even noticed Natalie was hiding in the corner.

The door opened behind her. In walked a short older black man, who she assumed was the doctor.

Bridgette I'esha

"How is he?" Sharnese asked in a soft whisper.

The man took a minute to examine Sharnese. Being a man of God, he wasn't one to judge, but he could tell they weren't living right. The wounds both obtained spoke volumes.

"I'm not going to promise a total recovery, but for the most part he should return to his normal self."

For some reason, Sharnese didn't believe him. She could hear the hesitation in his voice when he spoke.

"Exactly how much damage does he have?" She asked, already anticipating the worst.

"He was shot in his right shoulder, left chest, and twice in his lower back. The bullet just barely missed his heart. He's extremely blessed to even be alive right now." The doctor had left out some very important details on purpose. Hoping she wouldn't pry anymore.

"There's something you're not telling me. I can see it all on your face."

"Well...when he was shot in the back, one of the bullets landed in his spine."

"Can it be removed? Sharnese asked in a concerned manner.

"Right now, there's a strong possibility he may become paralyzed if we attempt to perform surgery." The doctor so badly wanted to tell her everything would be fine, but he wasn't in the business to make promises he couldn't keep.

No longer able to control her emotions, Sharnese let the tears flow freely. Grabbing Murda's free hand she placed it on her belly.

"Cortez, I know you're a strong fighter, and you'll get through this. We need you right now more than anything." Sharnese patiently waited for a response but received nothing. Guilt consumed her mind.

If only I wasn't being so stubborn, maybe we could have worked through our problems. Instead, my ass ran into the arms of another man who just happened to be his brother. What a fucked-up situation.

Sharnese attempted to get a response one last time before she gave up. "Just let me know you hear what I'm saying by at least blinking your eyes." Once again, a few minutes passed and still the same results. Overwhelmed by the events that had transpired for the day, Sharnese gathered what little strength she had left and prepared to leave.

The doctor could see the pain in her eyes as she stood by the door. It was always painful to watch someone see their loved ones suffer, especially when there's nothing they can do to take away the pain. Dr. Robinson was more than ever determined to help the young man heal. Many times, before he'd seen young black men lose their lives to the streets whether it be drug abuse or violence, and he was tired of it. In his soul, he could feel that the man was destined for greatness. God had a plan for him, and he wasn't finished just yet.

Natalie was still in the corner hiding, listening to every word that had been spoken. She wasn't sure how she felt now. One part of her felt sad and remorseful for Murda while the other part was bitter and envious of the fact that Sharnese was pregnant. She was determined Murda was going to be all hers. As long as she was alive sharing was not an option for her. *If Murda thinks it's going to be easy to get rid of me, then he better think again. He should have never given a crazy bitch like me some of that bomb ass dick*! Natalie thought to herself.

Natalie had deceived so many men with her precious baby face. When most men met her, they thought she was some shy, quiet chick, but that was not the case. They soon discovered her to be nothing more than a psychotic stalker chick. Once they got what they wanted from her and tried to break it off, she would stop at nothing to get revenge. There was no limit as to how far she would go to get even, and nobody was exempt. In her twisted mind, it was till death did them apart.

"Oh, Miss Sharnese, be prepared for your little world to come crumbling apart." Natalie hurriedly covered her mouth while looking around to make sure the doctor hadn't heard her. Thankfully he didn't. The last thing she wanted was to blow her cover. Visiting hours were bound to be over soon, and she wasn't trying to catch a trespassing charge, especially since she had open cases for stalking. In the meantime, she would continue to wait until the coast was clear.

*****

Sharnese had just gotten off the phone with Mama Peaches when the Emergency techs came rushing in with a badly beaten woman. For a minute, she stood there stuck. The girl favored her cousin Brooklyn, but she wasn't sure. Running down the hallway, she got another glance at the girl. Sure enough, it was Brooklyn. Sharnese wasn't sure what was going on, but she was going to find out. She could have sworn she'd heard the nurse say something about a drug overdose, but she knew that couldn't be true. All the years she'd known her cousin, the only thing she ever saw her do was smoke a little weed. The closer she got to the stretcher the more her chest began to heave in and out. Sharnese began hyperventilating. Her lungs were on fire, and she couldn't breathe. Beads of sweat formed on her forehead as her ears started to ring. Unable to keep her balance, she staggered to the nearest wall.

"Excuse me, Miss are you okay?" Asked a young black nurse who looked to be no older than twenty-eight years old. Sharnese couldn't even give the nurse a simple reply before her eyes started rolling to the back of her head. The nurse ran quickly to get a wheelchair. She made it back just in time. Sharnese fainted as soon as she sat down in the seat.

"Code Blue. Code Blue." The nurse shouted at the top of her lungs. It was no use in her announcing it over the intercom since she was already in the emergency room. Immediately doctors came running to her aid. Luckily Dr. Perez happened to be one of the doctors.

"Hurry and get an IV hooked up to her NOW! She's pregnant and from the complexion of her skin she looks to be extremely dehydrated." Whenever Dr. Perez came across an expecting patient, she made sure to take extreme precaution.

Once the fluid ran its course through her body, she slowly regained consciousness, but it didn't last long. Before she knew it, she'd drifted off into a deep sleep.

*****

After performing several tests on Brooklyn, the doctor had discovered a high amount of Heroin and Opium in her system. Two highly addictive drugs that were starting to become common in young adults. Being a veteran in the game, Dr. Perez had learned early on that you should never judge someone by their appearance. Although Brooklyn was suffering from an apparent overdose, she could tell it wasn't intentionally. It was very evident that she'd been drugged. To be on the safe side, she ordered a rape exam to be done. Her gut feeling was telling her that Brooklyn had been sexually assaulted. The bruises on her neck suggested that she'd been attacked violently.

What the hell is going on around here? This is the second victim I've encountered today where a young female has been violently abused. Sure, as my name is Angel Perez I will be getting

to the bottom of this. She thought.

Dr. Perez was good friends with a Detective down at Precinct 28. It wouldn't be hard for her to obtain information about her latest patient. Ever since her younger sister was murdered by her boyfriend, she made it her number one priority to help with Domestic Violence.

*****

Buzz! Buzz! Natalie jumped at the sound of her phone vibrating. Angel's name flashed across the screen. Unsure as to whether she wanted to answer the call, she let it go straight to voicemail. She knew that if it was important Angel would leave a message. The door made a loud thud as it closed.

"Fuck!" She screamed out loud. Finally, she was alone in the room with Murda. Walking around his bed, she took her hand and rubbed his face. As she looked at him she fought the urge to smother him with the pillow his head rested upon. All he had to do was answer her phone calls. Instead, he chose to ignore her which was the worst thing he could've done. Now, she was hell-bent on making his life a living hell.

Bridgette I'esha

"Mr. Rodriguez, you might as well take your last breath. It'll be much more painless, compared to what I have in store for you."

"I don't know who the hell you are, but you got five seconds to get your ass out of here before I put foot all in it," said a tired Destiny. The walk from the elevator had her breathless. Money stood behind her trying to figure out who the woman was. Something about her seemed familiar. He couldn't put his finger on it, but he'd seen her somewhere before.

"Are you threatening me?" Natalie asked. One thing she didn't take kindly to was threats. Natalie's temper was rising slowly. It took very little to get her pissed off.

"Don't leave and you will surely find out," Destiny threatened.

After Destiny said those last words, any professionalism Natalie had gone out the window. Standing toe to toe with Destiny in a low tone she whispered, "Try me." Before Money had a chance to intervene, Destiny had already swung landing a blow directly to Natalie's face. Natalie went to attack back but was stopped when Money grabbed a hold of her wrists.

"Not happening, not today." He didn't care that his wife was in the wrong. No matter what the situation was, he held her down like he was supposed to. There was no way he would let anyone do harm to her or their unborn child.

Seeing this was a battle she couldn't win, Natalie grabbed her purse and walked towards the door while eyeballing Destiny the entire time. "I will be seeing you one day," she said as she exited the room. Destiny had now made herself an enemy she would never forget.

"Damn it, Destiny! Have you forgot where your ass is at?" Money screamed at her. "We cannot afford to bring any unnecessary attention to you or Murda."

That quick she had forgotten that one altercation could've cost her everything. Since passing her Bar Exam a few months ago, she'd opened her own law firm, and it wasn't an easy process. But then again, nothing that you truly want ever comes easy. Many nights she wouldn't sleep at all because she was too busy studying trying to accomplish her dreams, and she'd done it. She graduated at the top of her class with not only her degree in Criminal Law but also her Master's Degree in Business.

Bridgette I'esha

"I'm sorry I overreacted. Shit, you know how protective I am about my best friend," she explained.

Destiny and Sharnese's friendship was like no other. They took the word loyalty to the heart. When they vowed to have each other's back it was something they took seriously, so of course, she got out of pocket when she saw an unknown female in her best friend's man face. Especially since Sharnese was not there to defend the situation herself.

Murda laid there with his eyes closed the entire time. His entire body was weak. Whenever he tried to alert them of him being conscious, he failed. He had heard the entire conversation between Sharnese and the doctor about his condition. He was determined to prove them both wrong. Any surgery that he needed to have then so be it. He refused to lay there and soak in self-pity. With his free hand, he hit the call button. "Ugh," he grunted as he tried to sit up on his own. The bright lights in the room put a strain on the one eye he could see out of causing him to fall back on the bed.

Money and Destiny both stopped talking when they noticed their friend was up. It was something neither of them was expecting so soon.

"Thank you, Jesus!" Destiny blurted out as she ran out of the room to get a doctor.

When the doctor entered the room, he smiled. Rarely did he see patients wake up out of a coma this quickly. He double checked his vitals. Everything was perfectly fine besides the bullet still in his spine. Slowly he began removing the tubes from his throat. He warned Murda that his throat would be a little sore and dry. He encouraged him to take deep breaths as he would experience a slight shortness of breath.

"Mr. Rodriguez, I want you to nod your head if you understand the questions I'm about to ask you. Okay?"

Murda slightly nodded his head up and down indicating that he understood.

"Do you know what happened to you?" Murda slowly shook his head up and down.

"Do you know who did this to you?"

Murda didn't respond.

The doctor fully understood it was a code of the streets not to snitch, so he didn't press the issue any further. Dr. Robinson felt that since he was alert and responding, he should go ahead and bring up the need for surgery. He also explained the possible outcome of the things that could go wrong.

Murda didn't care what the long-term effects would be. He just wanted to get better. He had faith that things would work out in his favor. His mind was telling him to give up his thuggish ways and go legit. Being in the streets had not only almost cost him his life, but also the love of his life. If surgery and recovery went as planned, then relocating him and Sharnese was next on his agenda.

"Go ahead and do it," Murda managed to say in between breaths.

"Are you sure? Take some time to think about this," said the doctor.

"Do it," Murda said again. This time in a much more persisted tone.

"That settles it then. I'll go and have the surgeon schedule you to have surgery in the next couple of hours until then get some rest."

Money wanted to interrogate him like the Detectives did on the "First 48", but decided against it. It had been one hell of a day for all of them, and the only thing he wanted was sleep.

Bridgette I'esha

"Man, you had us scared for a minute. Don't do that shit anymore. We thought you were gone, bruh." Money felt himself choking up. He didn't know what he would've done if he'd lost him.

"Kas is my blood brother," Murda blurted out.

"Them pain meds must got you higher than a muthafucka right now. Do you hear the shit you're saying?" Money said as he fell out laughing.

Murda looked at him with the sternest look he could give. "It's not a joke. He's Big Jimmy's son," he said. Immediately all of Money's laughter came to a halt He didn't know how to take the newly discovered information. This right here threw salt all in the game. It also left many questions in Murda's head. Does he seek revenge on his only brother? Or forgive him and try to make the situation, right?

Psshh! A puddle of clear liquid formed on the floor around Destiny's feet. Her water had just broken right there. "Money, it's time."

"You're right, it is time to go," he said not even noticing the change in Destiny's demeanor. He stepped right into the fluids when

Bridgette I'esha

he turned around. "The fuck Destiny! The bathroom is right back there."

"Nigga shut the hell up and get a doctor," she said as she doubled over in pain. The contractions started coming in back to back, and they were kicking her ass. Money just stood there. He was stuck. You would've thought it was his first rodeo the way he was acting. "Will you get a damn doctor?" Destiny screamed.

Money didn't even make it out the door before Dr. Robinson came running in. He'd heard the commotion in the hall and wanted to see what was going on. Destiny was rushed to the maternity ward where she gave birth to the most beautiful little girl ever, London Dior Williams. Money was overcome with joy. His family was now complete. He now had two Queens to protect and provide for. Destiny giving birth to their daughter made him love her even more. He knew then that he'd made the right choice by wanting to spend eternity with her.

"Hey, daddy's angel!" Money cooed as he held London in his arms. Her smile alone brightened up the entire room.

"Money put her down before you spoil her," Destiny said getting a tad bit jealous. She was used to being the only woman in his eyes. As London began to cry Money immediately handed her over to Destiny. Instantly Destiny's maternal instinct kicked in. As she rocked London back and forth, she settled down. The couple spent the next couple of hours bonding with their new addition.

*****

"Where am I?" Brooklyn asked in a groggy voice. The medication had finally worn off and slowly she was coming around.

Dr. Perez jumped at the sound of Brooklyn's voice. She was so caught up in her own thoughts. She wasn't paying any attention.

"You're in the hospital. You were found outside in front of the Emergency Room, suffering from a drug overdose," she explained.

Brooklyn's mind wandered thinking about the previous events that had taken place in the last twenty-four hours. She knew that her devious ways would catch up to her one day, but she had no idea she would be tortured in such ways. Her mind was dead set on getting revenge for everyone who had hurt her, and Mark was number one on her list. He may have been the one who saved her life, but he was also the one who had turned her over to Jean-Claude in the first place. Brooklyn didn't care that he killed Jean-Claude,

Mark was still going to die. A sinister grin appeared on her face as she imagined the agony she was going to put Mark through. She had devised a plan so ill, even the devil himself had to give her a pat on the back.

"So how long before this shit is out of my system? I got moves to make." It didn't take Brooklyn long to revert to her old ways. She wasted no time putting her plan into effect.

"From the looks of things, you're free to go about your business, but I would advise you to stay overnight to make sure all of the drugs have been flushed out of your system."

"Thanks, but no thanks," Brooklyn said as she rolled her eyes in her head. She didn't want to hear anything else the doctor had to say unless she was telling her how she could commit murder and get away with it.

Dr. Perez wanted to help Brooklyn, but she wasn't about to put up with her stank, nonchalant attitude in the process. If Brooklyn didn't care about her own well-being then why should she?

"Sit tight, I'll be right back with your discharge papers."

"Yeah, just hurry up already."

Dr. Perez bit her tongue and held her composure. Had she not been at work, she would've told Brooklyn about herself. It made her think twice about helping her, but she wasn't that kind of person. Her heart was too kind to even allow it.

Mama Peaches appeared in the room out of nowhere. Her heart sank when she saw the bruises on Brooklyn's face. As much as she wanted to feel sorry for her she couldn't. Too many times she had warned her that her ways would soon catch up with her. She couldn't do anything, but shake her head at the sight of her, relieved that her prayers had been answered. She might not have been in the best condition, but at least she was back where someone knew she was alive and well.

Where the hell did she come from? I'm not in the mood for her shit right about now. Brooklyn said to herself. One thing for sure, Mama Peaches knew exactly how to get under her skin. She didn't care what she said out of her mouth, or how deep she went. She was going to say what she wanted to whoever she wanted to say it to, and she didn't care how you felt afterward.

"Umph, you made it back home I see," Mama Peaches said with much attitude. "You could've called and let someone know where you were. You had us worried to death."

"Maybe I didn't want anyone to know my location."

Mama Peaches wanted to smack the piss out of her oldest granddaughter right there in the hospital. "It's time for you to get your shit together and start being a mother to your damn kids. When is the last time you've even spoken to any of them? You should feel less of a mother. Throwing four children off on someone else while you rip and run the streets."

Those words struck a nerve in Brooklyn. She loved all her kids to death, but the truth was she didn't know how to be a mother. She had become a mother when she was just a child herself. Her mother was never there to guide her along the way, so how could she be a mother or show love to her own children?

The doctor walked in with the discharge papers before Brooklyn had the chance to respond. "Here are your discharge papers with all of your instructions on them. Please be extremely careful and take care of yourself."

Brooklyn snatched the papers and left the room without saying a word to anybody. Mama Peaches and Dr. Perez just shook their heads as they looked at each other. They didn't understand how a girl could have so much attitude after being an inch away from death.

Chapter Two

Kas was sitting in the living room of his condo while "Doc", a street doctor, worked on his injured arm. The bullet had just grazed his shoulder, so it wasn't much work he had to have done. His body was numb to the pain as he thought about Murda being his brother and Big Jimmy being his father. He didn't give a fuck about any of that. Murda was going to get his. If Cain killed Abel what made anybody think that he wouldn't kill Murda? He would have to disappear for a while until he figured out how he would get at the nigga. He thought about paying him a visit while he was in the hospital but knew it would be too risky. Then again, he was the wild didn't give a fuck type.

"Yo Doc about how much longer you got?" Kas asked growing impatient. He was ready to make a few phone calls. He had some young comrades who were eager to eat, and ready to put in work. He planned on letting his man Jermaine handle most of the business while he got his head on straight.

"Not much longer," Doc replied. He hated people talking to him when he did his work. One fuck up could cost him his life. He'd been doing his job for over twenty years and hadn't had a mishap yet, and he wasn't about to have one now. Whenever the local dope boys or gang members found their selves messed up, they always found their way to Doc. It didn't matter the time of day or what he was doing. When them Benjamin's called he was on his way to them.

Grabbing the Hydrogen Peroxide from off the glass end table, he disinfected the wound one last time before wrapping the area with gauze. As tight as it was wrapped the bleeding was sure to stop at any second.

Kas paid Doc off and sent him on his way. He poured himself a shot of whiskey. The brown liquor did nothing but made him angry. The more he thought about Murda being his brother, the more he felt himself snapping. The resemblance was there. Until now he never realized how much he and Murda looked like twins. Deep down he wanted to forgive Murda and form a brother relationship with him, but his pride wouldn't let him do it. Or more so the streets wouldn't allow him to do it. He pulled out his phone and sent Jermaine a text stating he needed to speak with him.

Me: Meeting at my crib ASAP!

Maine: What's up cuz?

Me: Explain when you get here.

Maine: No problem.

Kas wasn't sure how he was going to explain the current situation at hand. Shit, he still had a hard time explaining it to himself. As the liquor began to kick in he thought about calling Chanel's thot ass. He needed someone to release his built-up frustration on.

Knock! Knock! His thoughts were interrupted by a knock at the door. It didn't take Jermaine any time to arrive at the house. Kas opened the door and greeted his right-hand.

"What's going on cuz?"

"You tell me," Jermaine replied.

"Shit is crazy cuz. Wait till I drop this one on you," Kas said as he ran his hand through his untamed hair.

"I'm listening."

"Check this, the nigga Murda is my brother yo. We got the same Pops. Some nigga named Jimmy."

Jermaine looked at Kas in disbelief. He didn't want to believe a thing his homie had just told him. Kas had never once lied to him, so he knew it had to be nothing but the truth. Jermaine wasn't one to be killing family, but this right here had him all fucked up.

"So how you plan on handling this?" Jermaine asked.

Kas sat there with a dumb expression written on his face. His mind was telling him all kinds of crazy shit but he kept it real with him. "Man Maine, I really don't know. One part of me is saying go split this nigga's wig all the way back while the other part of me is saying let that shit ride."

Jermaine respected his friend's honesty. He wouldn't know what he would've done if the shoe was on the other foot. It was easy to say what you would do until you were placed in the situation itself.

"Whatever decision you make, you know I'm riding with you," Jermaine reassured Kas.

Bridgette I'esha

"That's why I'm leaving you in charge for the time being. Re-ups and making sure everyone eats is all on you. I'm a have to take a mini vacation for a while."

"No problem cuz. You know I got you covered."

"Good looking homie." And just like that Jermaine walked right back out those doors.

*****

Weeks had passed by, and Murda was still in the hospital. His recovery was coming along fast. With surgery, the doctor removed the bullet with no permanent damage. Although it was taking quite some time for him to completely walk on his own with the physical therapy, he was receiving, every other part of his body was regaining its strength once again.

Every day Sharnese was there cheering him on. There were many days when Murda felt like giving up. Having to depend on others was not something he was used to. He often took his frustration out on Sharnese, which he didn't mean to.

"Come on Cortez you almost got it," Sharnese said as she encouraged him to finish his Physical Therapy session.

"I'm fucking trying Sharnese."

"Well, you're going to need to try a little harder if you plan on leaving this facility anytime soon," Dr. Robinson chimed in.

"Ugh," Murda let out a loud grunt with each step he took. His walking distance had increased tremendously since the last time he'd completed the exercise. Taking a few more steps, this time he pushed the walker to the side. Standing up straight he walked to the front of the room with no support. Surprisingly he wasn't even out of breath.

The doctor watched in astonishment. Every day he would increase the intensity of the workouts on purpose. From the day that he'd met Murda, he knew that he would overcome the obstacles in his way. "Good job Mr. Rodriguez!" He said clapping his hands together applauding his progress. "I must say I'm very impressed with the self-determination you have."

"Does this mean he can come home?" Sharnese asked.

"If he continues to walk alone like this, then come the end of the week I'm pretty sure he'll be able to leave." Sharnese ran over to the doctor and gave him a hug. This was the news she'd been waiting on for weeks.

"Oh my God, I got so much to prepare for in so little time." Sharnese was more excited than a kid on Christmas Day. "Oh yeah that reminds me," she said as she handed Murda an unopened envelope. The results of his and Chanel's paternity test had come in the mail. It was killing her not knowing what the papers said. As much as she wanted to hate Chanel she couldn't. It was Murda she should hate. If he had never stepped out on their relationship in the first place, then they would not have been going through so much drama.

"In the case of two-month-old Elijah Rodriguez...Cortez, you are not the father!" Murda shouted. He was sure everyone in the building heard him reading the results. He had just dodged a major bullet.

Good news has been coming my way. I was happier than a muthafucka to know that Chanel's son wasn't mine. There was no way in hell I would be able to deal with her ignorant ass for the next eighteen years. This calls for a celebration when I get home. A blunt of loud got my name written all over it somewhere. Murda thought.

"Well, I'll leave you two to celebrate alone. I have other patients to tend to."

Murda and Sharnese thanked Dr. Robinson once again before he left the room. Murda took a moment to take in Sharnese's appearance. She looked a little different compared to a few months ago. Her face had a glow to it, and her hips had gotten a little wider. His eyes narrowed down on her stomach, and that's when he noticed the pudge underneath the big T-shirt she had on.

"You pregnant?" Murda asked already knowing the answer to the obvious.

Sharnese was caught completely off guard. She rubbed her stomach and smiled. "Yes, we are. I mentioned it to you weeks ago while you were in the coma." She tried to read Murda's facial expression, but there was none. Then a huge smiled formed on his face.

"Sharnese you just made me the happiest man on Earth," Murda said as he pulled her in for a kiss. The soft sensation of his lips pressed against hers caused her body to tense up. It had been a long time since she'd felt any type of affection from the man she dearly loved. Closing the blinds and making sure the door was locked, Sharnese gently pushed Murda down onto the stool. She was yearning to feel his stiff penis inside of her. The more they passionately kissed the more her juice box began to flow. Down on all fours, she pulled Murda's Red and Black basketball shorts down to his ankles. She licked the shaft of his dick slowly before spitting on it, making it wet.

Murda sat there shocked. He had never seen this side of Sharnese before. Normally, when they had intercourse he was the one to take charge, but he wasn't complaining one bit. His toes curled as Sharnese bobbed her head up and down. She was sucking the life out of his man, and balls at the same time. Her head game was unexplainable. He ran his fingers through her hair as she continued to go down on him. Murda flinched as he felt himself about to release his seeds down her throat. He tapped her shoulder so she could stop. Sharnese got up and wrapped her legs around his hips as she straddled him tightly. Rocking back and forth in a slow motion Murda grabbed hold of her hips. Her body was in complete ecstasy as she called out his name.

"Damn, I missed this dick," she said picking up the pace.

"Slow down Nese. You gon make me nut fast," Murda said trying to hold off a little longer. Sharnese was too gone to slow down. She was on the verge of reaching her peak.

Bridgette I'esha

"Cum with me babe. I'm ready to cum."

He gave the biggest thrust he could before both of their bodies began to shake. A knock at the door made their hearts pound even faster. Sex was always the best when you were sneaking around. They hurriedly fixed their clothes as Sharnese ran to open the door.

"Hey Mama Peaches and Mrs. Carmen," Sharnese said a little jittery.

"Hey baby," Mama Peaches said in return.

"Honey, I done told you plenty of times before you can call me Mom," Carmen said to Sharnese

Mama Peaches and Carmen both looked at each other with the strangest look on their faces. Sharnese looked around in confusion. She didn't know why the two had that look on their faces. Mama Peaches searched around in the bathroom until she found exactly what she was looking for. Walking back out she sprayed the Glade Apple Cinnamon Air freshener.

"Much better. You two could've at least sprayed when you were done."

"Huh?" Sharnese said.

Bridgette I'esha

"Don't play dumb my dear. The smell of ass is all in the air."
Everyone busted out into laughter. Mama Peaches didn't care what she said out of her mouth. Sharnese's cheeks flushed red in embarrassment. She quickly changed the subject.

"So, what brings you all by?"

"We were just out shopping for the newest addition to the family," Carmen answered for them both.

"And don't you try and deny it either Sharnese Jackson. It's written all over your face," Mama Peaches said.

Damn, it never fails. This woman always knows when something is up. She probably knows when I have to piss too.
Sharnese thought to herself. "I wasn't going to deny it. I was just waiting for the right time to tell everyone. And how are you two out buying things when you don't even know the gender of the baby?"

"It's a boy. The glow you have developed says it all," replied Carmen. The two older women continued with their old midwives' theories until Sharnese got up to excuse herself.

"Well, I hate to end this little session, but I must get going."

"You aren't the only one," Carmen said picking up her all-black Michael Kor's purse. "I still have to go home and prepare

Bridgette I'esha

dinner." Everyone said their goodbyes as they went their separate ways.

*****

Carmen was in their enormous kitchen preparing Big Jimmy's favorite meal of curry chicken with carrots and huge chunks of white potatoes, along with some white rice, and sweet fried bread. Although they had a personal chef, Carmen preferred to cook her own meals sometimes. It was nothing like having a home cooked meal from the heart. Carmen took a few sips from her glass of red wine as she sang along with her girl Mary.

Yeah, we disagree, fuss and fight, we get it wrong more

Then it's right.

Yeah, we make mistakes, and fix mistakes but never even

Seeing eye to eye

But when the dust clears it's settled, and it's all said and
done.

When the night breaks and day finally comes...

Will you love me in the morning?

After the evening will you need me?

Now that the suns up will you give up?

Bridgette I'esha

Mary J. Blige did the damn thing when she sang that song.
Carmen thought to herself as she reminisced about her younger years
with Jimmy. Things had not always been perfect with the two.
Jimmy had shown her he could be a better man. She often wondered
how things would've been if she'd never met Jimmy, but she couldn't
imagine life without the man who had taken her from off the streets.

Jimmy smiled at the sight of Carmen fixing one of his
favorite meals. She was everything he could have asked for in a wife.
At times he knew he didn't deserve her. There were plenty of times
when Carmen had caught him cheating with several different women,
and each time she would make an example out of them. After that,
most of the women in New York got the picture that he was off
limits. They were just about to sit down and devour their dinner
when the doorbell rang.

Ding dong…Ding dong. The bell rang repeatedly. Whoever
was at the door was clearly not leaving until someone answered the
door.

"Somebody wants a cap put in their ass." Everyone knew
better than to show up at his house unannounced. When he opened

Bridgette I'esha

the door, he was speechless. There stood Diana a woman he hadn't laid eyes on in years.

"Honey, who's at the door," Carmen asked. It was taking him a long time to respond. "Jimmy, who's there?" The awkward silence was not sitting well with her. Removing her apron, she made her way into the living room. She blinked her eyes a couple of times to ensure she wasn't seeing things. Nope. Diana was standing there at her house in the flesh. It took everything in Carmen not to lose her cool. She wanted to hear everything this bitch had to say.

Diana turned her nose up at the sight of Carmen. After these years, she still couldn't accept the fact that Jimmy chose her.

"Diana, what are you doing here?" Jimmy asked in a very pissed off tone. He blamed her for the ongoing war between his two sons. If she would've contacted him about their son, then he could've stopped the war from the very beginning.

"I want to talk to you about our son," Diana said as she tapped her foot on the Marble tiled floor.

"You got a lot of nerve bringing your ass to our home," Carmen said not giving Jimmy a chance to respond.

"Babe, let me handle this," Jimmy said as he rubbed her lower back attempting to calm her down.

"You got it, but one wrong move and bitch it's your ass," she said staring Diana directly into her eyes. Diana knew Carmen wouldn't hesitate to whip her ass, so she kept her smart comments to herself for the time being.

"Because of you, I have two sons out here trying to kill each other. Twenty-seven years later and now you want to talk. I don't think we have anything to talk about. Tell my son if he has any questions he wants answered to give me a call. Now get your ass off my property before I have you arrested for trespassing," Jimmy said as he slammed the door in Diana's face.

Carmen stood there with a grin on her face. She was just about to make a comment when he stopped her. "Carmen not right now. I already got enough on my mind as it is. I don't need you making it any worse." She saw that he wasn't in the mood for her foolishness, so she left him alone.

"Go have a seat out back and I'll bring your plate and a beer."

"Thanks," Jimmy said as he made his way around back.

*****

Bridgette I'esha

Brooklyn sat in the driveway of her home. She hadn't been there in months. There was no trace of blood on the door like she last remembered, and she had no idea who had gotten rid of the body. Nor did she care. She was just glad it was gone. There had been no reports on the news about the murder. She figured they just wrote it off as a robbery gone bad.

Brooklyn took her time as she made her way through her home. Everything was still the same way she'd left it. She began straightening up a little. The smell of the molded pizza had caused a strong stench in the air. Putting on a pair of latex gloves she poured some bleach and hot water into a bucket and went to work scrubbing. Throwing all the trash into the garbage bag she was surprised by how much energy she had. Wiping off the counters she paused when she came to a picture of her children. Jordan, Domonique, Raven, and Sincere were her world. She needed to hear their voices. She found her Aunt Caroline's number in the contacts section of her phone and pressed send.

"Hello?"

"Hello? Aunt Caroline?" Brooklyn asked in between sniffles.

"Brooklyn dear is that you?" Her aunt asked unsure.

Bridgette I'esha

"Yes, it's me," she replied.

"Baby there's no need to explain your absence. I already talked to your grandmother, and she filled me in somewhat." That's why Brooklyn loved her Aunt. No matter how much trouble she stayed in, or how she lived her life her aunt never once judged her for it.

"Hold on for a second while I put you on speakerphone." She struggled for a few minutes trying to figure out how to work her iPhone. "Brooklyn baby are you there?"

"Yes Auntie, I'm still here."

"You know us old folks have a time trying to work this new crap they got." Brooklyn laughed. It was something she hadn't done in a while. "Raven and Sincere come talk to your mother." She yelled into the background.

"Mommy! We miss you!" Brooklyn's youngest two kids shouted into the phone.

"I miss you all too! Where are Jordan and Domonique?" Brooklyn questioned.

"They walked to the corner store to grab some snacks," Caroline replied while looking at the clock. "They should be on their way back."

"You let them walk alone?" Brooklyn asked. She had forgotten that her oldest son Jordan was eleven-years-old.

"Yes, the store is less than ten minutes away. You know I wouldn't let anything happen to those precious babies."

"I know Aunt Caroline, I'll be down there in the next couple of weeks to visit," Brooklyn said.

"That'll be great."

Brooklyn was cleaning the side of her windows when she noticed Mark's car pulling into her driveway.

"Aunt Caroline I hate to cut this conversation short, but I have to go. Kiss my babies for me and have them call me sometime tomorrow."

"No problem, take care of yourself and be careful out there," she said as she ended the call.

Brooklyn stared out the window for a few more seconds before proceeding to the door. "What are you doing here? And how do you know where I live?" She questioned Mark as he got out of his car.

Mark didn't know how Brooklyn was going to react once she saw him. He wanted to stay at the hospital with her the day he dropped her off, but he knew the doctors and police were sure to take him in for questioning. "I got your address from your license," he said.

"So, you went through my belongings?" Brooklyn asked.

"Didn't you get caught going through mine?" Mark answered her question with a question of his own.

"I'm asking the questions here not you." She reminded him. For a minute, she found herself forgiving him, but as quickly as it crossed her mind it left. In her eyes, this man was responsible for her near-death experience. She could've become addicted to heroin and for that, she couldn't forgive him.

"Will you forgive me?" Mark asked with pleading eyes. "I never knew what my Uncle was going to do to you."

Brooklyn stood there and rolled her eyes. She believed his story about not knowing, but it was the fact that he turned her over in the first place. That she couldn't get passed.

"Then why did you do it?" She just had to know. "What was in it for you?"

"Honestly it was all about the money...But once I saw what was being done to you, I regretted ever handing you over."

"You're full of shit." *I may have been doped up during most of it, but he's not about to stand here and insult my intelligence. His dumb ass was just mad that he got played like a lil bitch. He received no money in return for his services.*

"If you say so."

"Look you were interrupting my cleaning time. So, unless you plan on helping me clean, I'm going to need you to vacate the premises," Brooklyn said as she turned around. She was growing tired of the back and forth game they were playing.

"Show me what needs to be done and I'll be more than glad to help." Mark smiled showing his pearly whites. He placed his long dreads into a tight ponytail as he entered the house. Brooklyn handed him the mop and bucket while showing him where all the cleaning supplies were located.

"I need my entire house cleaned spotless. From top to bottom, and front to back. Any dirty clothes you find laying around you can

Bridgette I'esha

throw them in the washer. I also need my carpet shampooed when you're done. I have a few errands to run so I'll be back in a couple of hours and please don't disappoint me," Brooklyn said with a straight face.

Mark should've known she was dead serious when she came with a bunch of cleaning supplies. *Damn, I didn't think she was going to put a nigga to work like this. I might as well get it done. It's the least I can do.*

Brooklyn got into her car and made her way to *Dazzlin Diamonds.* She wanted to talk to Ricky about possibly getting her job back until she found something more suitable. Everyone greeted her as if she'd fallen off the face of the earth. She saw a couple of new dancers, who looked at her funny. Brooklyn didn't care though. She knew it was a wrap once the men found out that she was back in town.

She spotted Ricky in the face of some obviously young amateur dancer. The girl didn't even look old enough to be dancing in anyone's club. But none the less, it wasn't any of her business. She'd once been that same girl looking for a way to earn a few extra bucks.

"Excuse me, honey. Do you mind if I borrow him for a few minutes?" Brooklyn asked the young girl. The girl nodded her head relieved to be getting Ricky out of her face. Brooklyn watched the girl as she walked away wondering what her story was. If Brooklyn didn't know anything else, she knew that stripping would either make you or break you.

"Paradise, is it?" Ricky asked attempting to play mind games with Brooklyn only she didn't feed into it. She was not the same Brooklyn from months ago.

"Let's skip all the small talk, shall we? I just came here to get my job back," Brooklyn said getting straight to the point. There was money to be made, and she wanted in. She was just trying to make enough money to get back on her feet. Once she got what she needed, her next plan would involve her getting her children back.

"You can have your job back, but only under certain conditions. You will pay for stage fees on time like all the rest of the dancers, and you will have to start at the bottom working during the week. You also have to earn your way back to opening on weekends.

"No problem," Brooklyn said very confidently. She knew once her regular customers found out she was back they would be lined up at the door waiting to see her perform. After wrapping up her conversation with Ricky, Brooklyn walked around the club to check out her competition. None of the girls had anything that stood out about them. All of them were pretty much basic. They all did the same tired moves on the stage. Bending over making their asses clap, and all that other shit. Even their costumes were tired. Brooklyn continued about her business until she made her way to the dressing room. Surprisingly it was empty, besides the one girl she'd seen talking to Ricky earlier. Her head was in between her hands while she cried out loud. Brooklyn started to turn around and walk straight out, but something about the girl said she needed help.

I need to take my ass right back out those doors. I'm the last person who needs to be helping anybody. Especially when I don't have my own shit together.

"You good?" Brooklyn yelled out to the girl.

Yarley slowly lifted her head up. Since she had started working there, none of the girls had said one word to her. Her black mascara ran down her face, and her eyes were red and puffy from crying.

"Why are you being nice to me?" Yarely asked. She rarely got along with other females. They always hated her for no reason at all. She stood at 5'11 weighing in at 180 lbs. of solid weight. She had Green eyes and a long red weave. It was no denying that she was a very pretty girl. Her skin was so light most people would've considered her to be high yellow.

"I don't know you seem lost. How old are you?" Brooklyn asked taking a seat beside her.

"Eighteen in a few weeks," Yarley replied.

"Oh, my! You're just a baby." Brooklyn's heart went out to the young girl. She was just sixteen when she was introduced to this lifestyle.

"I don't know your reasons for being here and it isn't any of my business, but I will say this, get your money and get out. Go to college or whatever it is you plan on doing, but do not make a career out of this. I'm telling you. You'll find yourself doing shit you'd never imagine doing in a million years just for a little piece of money. For what? To keep your hair, and nails done. An outfit here, and a bag there. In the end, you'll see that it's not worth it, trust me." Brooklyn stood up ready to leave.

Bridgette I'esha

Yarely stopped her with one question on her mind. "Why did you come back?" Yarely asked. She had heard plenty of stories about Paradise, but it was hard for her to believe any of them.

"The same reason you're here. I need the money," she said walking out of the door.

*****

Brooklyn returned home surprised to see that Mark's car was still in her driveway. When she walked inside, her mouth dropped. Mark had literally cleaned her house all over. He had even lit some strawberry candles throughout the entire house. A smell ran across her nose, and she followed it towards the kitchen. Mark had manifested an entire meal. Fresh from the oven were some baked Turkey wings, smothered in onion gravy, with some homemade mashed potatoes, green beans, and honey yeast rolls. Brooklyn's mouth watered at the site of the food. It had been a minute since she had a home-cooked meal. She didn't say anything as she washed her hands to fix a plate.

"What bitch did you have over my house cooking dinner?" She asked. There was no way he could've cooked food this good.

"Nobody, I cooked the entire meal myself," Mark assured her.

Brooklyn looked at him out the corner of her eye. She had never met a man with skills in the kitchen. "Okay, I guess I'll go ahead and give you, ya props then."

After they were finished eating, Brooklyn and Mark both cleaned the dishes. Brooklyn was getting tired and needed some rest. She had to pretty much threaten to call the police to get Mark to leave. She told him she would give him a call the next day as she showed him to the door. Lying back on her king-sized bed she didn't even make it to take a shower before she ended up sleeping the night away.

Chapter Three

Sharnese had just gotten off the phone with the catering company. She was putting together the final touches for Murda's welcome home party. Her growing belly stood out in her pink wife beater. Nowadays she barely kept any clothes on due to always being warm. Her hormones were definitely out of whack during this pregnancy.

She couldn't wait to finally have Murda back home with her. Since the results of the paternity test had come back, the two were trying very hard to fix their relationship. It wasn't an easy process for Sharnese to forgive him. She was always going to have her insecurities. As crazy as it seemed, Sharnese felt like they were the perfect match for one another. Although Murda had cheated, he always showed her the utmost respect. You could tell he was raised by a Queen with the way he treated Sharnese.

Sharnese took a minute to reflect on her life. Things were going great, and most importantly she was happy. She had even started to develop a relationship with her mother. It wasn't easy forgiving her mother for all the pain she had caused her, but by the grace of God, they've been attending Church together on Sundays and things were looking up. They were even thinking about attending a few family therapy sessions together. Sharnese just wanted things right before she brought her own child into this cold world.

She looked at the time and saw she was late for a lunch date with Destiny. They had agreed to meet at the local park. Since all the events had transpired they hadn't been able to talk like they normally did. Sharnese locked up the house and headed over to Central Park.

*****

Destiny knew she had to have looked at her watch a thousand times. She started to call Sharnese and make sure she was okay but decided not to when she saw her walking up the sidewalk.

"It took ya ass long enough," Destiny said making sure baby London was fastened properly in her stroller. Destiny was a first-time mother with bad nerves. She always thought something was

Bridgette I'esha

going to happen to London no matter where she was at. Her biggest fear was an enemy or crazy client kidnapping her precious baby girl.

"And you're one to complain when normally ya ass is the one always late. Don't just sit there and look cute, bitch give me a hug!" The two hugged like they were long lost, friends. No matter how long they went without speaking, there was no questioning their loyalty. They both understood they had their own families to look after.

"So, what's been going?" Sharnese asked Destiny as she played with London. She had to admit she was the most gorgeous baby she'd ever seen. She had the fattest cheeks ever, and all Sharnese wanted to do was pinch them.

"Nothing much, just the usual." Destiny knew it was a reason she wanted to speak with Sharnese in person, but couldn't remember what it was. She picked off a piece of bread from her ham & cheese sandwich and threw it at the birds. It was just something she always wanted to try, just to see their reaction.

"Same here, just preparing for Murda's welcome home party."

"That reminds me. When I was at the hospital some strange female was in his room with him up close and personal. We ended up coming to blows right there in the room." Destiny paused for a minute trying to choose her next set of words wisely. "Something just wasn't right about her. Money swears he's seen her before but doesn't remember where. But don't worry I'm doing my own private investigation as we speak."

Sharnese smiled. She knew her girl would always come through for her. She wasn't going to say anything to Murda about it until she had the full scoop on shawty. On the inside, she hoped there wasn't anything else he'd done to put their relationship on the line again. Sharnese thanked Destiny for the information, and they took a short walk around the park before it started to rain. It was hilarious seeing Destiny running in the rain, pushing a stroller, especially since she was always concerned about messing up her hair.

*****

Everyone was gathered in the backyard, mingling and having a good time. There was plenty of food and an unlimited supply of alcohol. To Murda, it felt good having all his loved ones around, but for some reason, he was distant from everyone. Physically he was there in the flesh, but mentally his mind was someplace else.

For the past couple of days, he'd been receiving strange phone calls from an out of area number. To say he was stressed would've been an understatement. The only person that came to his mind was Natalie. Before she'd been blowing his line up nonstop, but now shit was getting out of hand. He didn't know how much longer he could keep the mysterious phone calls a secret. He knew he would have to come clean and tell Sharnese about Natalie. He just hoped it wouldn't put another strain on their relationship, especially since things were finally getting back on track.

"Hey Bae, why you over here by yourself?" Sharnese asked while taking in a forkful of Pasta Salad. It was her biggest craving so far.

Murda wasn't trying to mess up the mood so he quickly replied. "No real reason. Just admiring your beauty from a distance."

Sharnese blushed. The compliment made her feel good about herself. Since picking up a few pounds, she'd become self-conscious.

"Thank you, bae. I really needed to hear that," she said looking down at the ground. Murda instantly sensed something was bothering her. She was never this quiet.

"What's wrong?" He asked rubbing his hand on her lower back.

"Just glad to have you home," Sharnese smiled. "Now let's go and enjoy our guests."

*****

A couple of hours had gone by. It was well after eleven o'clock at night and everyone was still partying and carrying on. Mama Peaches and Tonya were in the middle of the yard having a "twerk contest" off of Too Short's *Shake Dat Monkey*. The Peach Ciroc along with the cups of Kinky had them turnt all the way up! Sharnese was getting restless. She was ready for everyone to go home.

Grabbing the microphone from the D.J. who was shouting "Turn down for what!" She made an announcement.

"I would like to thank all of you for coming out to celebrate Murda's return home, but it's time for you all to get the hell up out of here!" Everyone laughed at Sharnese's sense of humor. After saying her goodbyes, she looked at the mess that was left behind.

"I got it," Destiny said noticing the look Sharnese had on her face.

"Are you sure?" Sharnese asked. She hated putting her company to work whenever they came over.

"Yes, I'm fine. Go ahead and get some rest. Money and I will clean up. We got this," Destiny assured her as she pushed her inside the house. Sharnese looked around for Murda but saw no signs of him. Peeking out the window she spotted him helping Money clean up.

Good, this gives me enough time to get ready. Sharnese proceeded to walk up the stairway. She still had one last surprise for Murda.

Meanwhile, the two men were stacking the white chairs on top of one another. Murda was telling Money about the mysterious phone calls he'd been receiving.

"Man, I'm telling you it's the fucking realtor playing these dumb ass games on my shit. Ever since I gave shawty the pipe she's been calling me like crazy," Murda said slamming the chairs with a little too much force. "I ain't never in my life met a bitch that was so pressed for some dick."

Money chuckled. Here lately Murda stayed in some shit when it came to females. "That's what ya ass get for mixing business and pleasure in the first place. You knew it was bound to be some shit when you're fucking a bitch that's handling ya money. What the fuck was you thinking?"

"If you had seen the way her ass was moving in that thin sundress she had on, even you would've reconsidered being faithful to Destiny."

Money ignored the last part of Murda's comment. His dick was strictly for his wife. He didn't even give other women the time of day. It didn't matter where he was, he always spoke highly of her.

"This has got to be the bitch that was at the hospital, bruh."

Murda had a weird look on his face as he looked at Money. "What you are talking about bruh?" Murda asked getting serious. He hated when people talked in circles. *If this nigga knows something, then I'ma need for him to start talking. Murda thought.*

"Long story short, there was some mixed looking broad in your room while you were in the hospital. Destiny and the bitch ended up scrapping right there in the hospital room. I had to remind Destiny about the type of dealings we have." Money shook his head as he remembered the entire scene. "I ain't gon lie bruh. She pissed me off by pulling a stunt like that in the hospital."

Now that it was confirmed to be Natalie, Murda knew he had to get rid of her before she became a bigger problem. "Good looking bruh. Now I got to get rid of this crazy bitch. Ain't no telling how things would've gone down if Sharnese had been there."

"You know I got you," Money said as him and Murda dapped each other up.

*****

Murda didn't know what was going on when he entered their master bedroom. Sharnese had vanilla scented candles lit throughout the entire room. Murda inhaled the scent. He was a firm believer that aromatherapy helped to soothe the mind and relieve stress. On the bed were red and white rose petals shaped into a heart. Inside the heart sat a small velvet gift box, and a silver diamond encrusted picture frame. The picture was when they had first met in Jamaica. Murda smiled as he reminisced about their first encounter.

Sharnese appeared in the doorway wearing a red and black negligée and a pair of red bottom pumps. Her hair was styled into a medium length bob. It made her exotic looks standout even more. Adina Howard's *T-shirt and Panties* flowed in the background.

Murda had to admit, Sharnese looked damned good standing there like she was *America's Next Top Model.* At that moment, Sharnese was lost as she swayed her hips back and forth to the rhythm of the music. Murda was just about to make a comment when Sharnese placed her fingers to his lips signaling him to remain silent.

"Sshh," she said as she traced the outline of his juicy lips with her super long tongue.

"I just want to show how much I appreciate you. I know things were rocky between us, but I'm glad we're making it through the stormy weather." She blinked her eyes a couple of times to stop from crying.

Damn Sharnese get it together. She said in her head, giving herself a small pep talk. She'd always had a problem expressing her feelings and her being extra emotional wasn't making it any better. After taking a minute to get herself together she continued.

Bridgette I'esha

"Thank you for giving me a chance to experience love. Something I never thought I would be able to do." She really loved everything about the man in front of her eyes.

Murda ran his muscular hands along her thighs. Her entire body shivered at the sensation of his touch. Her body was yearning for him to fulfill her every need and fantasy. Murda was a man who loved to have control of a situation. To him, it portrayed a sign of weakness by letting a woman take charge. It was uncomfortable allowing Sharnese cater to him.

Murda returned the gesture by diving head first into her crotch. Sharnese always had the freshest vagina. So, he never minded pleasing her orally. The more he sucked on her clit, the more she creamed. Murda continued to slurp away catching every drop of her wetness. Her juices covered his entire face as she popped her coochie back and forth. Sharnese took one of her breasts into her mouth and flicked her tongue around her nipples.

"Oh shit! Right there Murda!" She hollered out in excitement. On the verge of climaxing, she pushed his head away from her love box. She was ready to feel him inside of her already. Murda laid Sharnese flat on her stomach. Being careful not to cause her any pain in the process. Slowly he entered her from behind. He tightly held onto her wide hips. Sharnese let out a slight moan as Murda's penis filled her vagina to its full capacity. They explored each other's bodies until the wee hours of the next morning.

Even after hours of steaming hot sex Murda's mind was still spaced out. He wouldn't be at peace until he told Sharnese about Natalie.

"Yo Nese, you sleep?" He called out to Sharnese while nudging her in the side.

"If I was sleep, ya ass done woke me up, shit. What you want?" She asked in a grouchy voice. She hated to be awakened out of her sleep unless it was an emergency.

"I need to rap with you about some shit real quick." Murda had her undivided attention. "While we were on our break," he paused before carrying on, "I fucked this bitch one time, and now she's stalking me and shit."

"What exactly do you mean by stalking you?" Sharnese asked making sure she understood every word that he spoke out of his mouth.

"Steady calling my phone. I even think she came to visit me while I was in the hospital," he said making sure he didn't leave anything out.

"If it was during our breakup, then we should be getting rid of this bitch ASAP." Murda loved Sharnese's gangsta side. She only displayed it when necessary. She wasn't the loud ghetto type of female. She always presented herself with class. Not a person that walked this earth could say they'd seen Sharnese get out of pocket for no apparent reason. "Since we're having this conversation is there anything else I need to know about?" Sharnese asked Murda with a serious ass look on her face while staring into his pretty eyes. She didn't want to be hit with any more surprises.

"Nah, that's it baby girl. I just want you to focus on bringing my son into this world healthy. I'll take care of the rest."

"There you go with that son stuff. How you and everybody else know it's not our daughter that I'm carrying?" Sharnese said with her lips poked out.

"Boy or girl, I don't care as look as it's healthy."

His ass just better concentrate on getting rid of this Natalie bitch or else I'ma have to come out of retirement and rock this bitch to sleep myself.

"Oh yeah, I almost forgot, there is one more thing I need to ask you," Murda said with a big Kool-Aid smile on his face.

"Boy, why you smiling so hard? Looking silly!" Sharnese said. She couldn't stop herself from laughing.

"Sharnese Jackson, will you hold me down for life? Are you ready to accept your title as the first lady?" Murda asked her while flashing a beautiful 14 Karat White-Gold Three-Stoned engagement ring.

Sharnese hollered out, "Yes," while waving her hand in his face. Murda placed the ring on her finger and stared at his wife to be. After having his heart broken plenty of times before, he'd finally felt it coming back together again.

Sharnese felt like the happiest woman in the world. They continued their sexcapade until they fell asleep in each other's arms.

Chapter Four

Kas rode through the streets of Brooklyn searching for anyone he thought was a part of Murda's crew. He had made up his mind to go ahead and kill Murda. It didn't matter to him that they shared the same father. Hell, he didn't even know the man who helped create him. Kas's ringing phone startled him. It was his mother calling. He pressed the ignore button and focused back to the task at hand. Kas hadn't spoken to his mother in weeks. He was trying his hardest to understand her reasoning for lying to him about who his father was. It wasn't like he was the little boy who always cried for his father. No, he was a grown ass man who deserved to know the truth.

"Fuck! Where are these fucking niggas hiding at?" He said to no one. Block after block he drove around with his blue bandana hanging out the driver's window being straight disrespectful. He wasn't afraid to show his colors no matter where he went. He was just about to go in for the night when he spotted a bad ass brown skinned chick that he had to have.

"Aye Shawty, let me holler at ya for a minute," Kas waited for a reply as he pulled up to the sidewalk next to where Brooklyn was walking.

Brooklyn turned around to see who was talking to her. Instantly her eyes saw a come-up. She had only been back to work for a month or so now, and already she was tired of it. The money wasn't coming in fast enough for her, and she was over the attitudes and drama from the other dancers in the club.

Brooklyn put an extra bounce in her walk as she made her way over to the Black 2016 Mercedes Benz S550. "You talking to me?" Brooklyn asked already knowing the answer.

"Yeah, hop in so we can talk some more."

Brooklyn looked at him like he was crazy. "I don't know about all that. My mama told me to never get into cars with strangers!"

Bridgette I'esha

Kas laughed at her like she'd just told the funniest joke ever. "Well, maybe, you can help me find my brother." Kas showed Brooklyn a picture of Murda on his phone. Brooklyn stared at the picture like she was in deep thought.

"I know him that's my cousin's man," Brooklyn said not certain about what was really going on.

Jackpot! This shit is too easy. Maybe she'll want in on this once in a lifetime opportunity. "You and ya cuz real close or something?" He asked digging for more information.

"Man fuck that uppity bitch," Brooklyn said with jealousy written all over her face. Ever since Sharnese and Murda had become a couple, Brooklyn hadn't heard much from her. In Brooklyn's mind, Sharnese thought she was better than her. Now, in her eyes, Sharnese was no better than anyone else who crossed her path.

"Oh, it's like that between y'all. Well, how about I put you in on a chance to earn some cash?" He asked.

"Exactly how much you are talking?" Brooklyn asked trying to figure out what she was getting herself into. Right, then Brooklyn didn't care what the job consisted of. She needed the money. "Well you can count me in, but there's one thing."

"What's that?" Kas asked.

"I'm a need a small cash deposit up front."

"No problem," Kas said as he ran the entire game plan down to Brooklyn. She didn't care about anything Kas was saying. Her mind was on the money only. Sharnese may have been blood, but even family turned out to be frenemies. Kas and Brooklyn exchanged numbers and went their separate ways. Kas still had to make a stop at the trap house and bust a few licks. He sent Jermaine a text letting him know he was about to swing through.

This nigga is a damn fool if he thinks for a second I'm a turn my blood in for some money. He should've done a background check on who I was before he decided on making death arrangements. Brooklyn placed a call to Sharnese on her Samsung Note.

"Hello?" Sharnese answered on the first ring.

"Long time, no talk," Brooklyn replied into the phone. "I'm a get straight to the point. I need to speak to you and Murda in private sometime soon."

"You can stop by now if it's that important," Sharnese said wondering what Brooklyn had to speak to them about. She knew nothing, but bad luck came from dealing with her cousin. It was like she was cursed or something.

"Alright, I'm leaving the club as we speak. Give me about twenty minutes and I'll be there."

"I'll see you when you get here then."

Brooklyn ended the call. She was just about to leave in her car when she was blocked in by Money and right beside him sat Destiny. Money was the first to step out of the car. He wasn't in the mood for any of Brooklyn's bullshit. He just wanted to know when his son would be returning.

"When is Sincere coming back?" Money asked not even bothering to acknowledge her.

"Well damn, no hey how you doing, or Brooklyn kiss my ass? What you can't speak because ya bitch with you?"

Money felt his blood beginning to boil. Brooklyn knew better than to disrespect Destiny in front of him. All he asked was a simple question pertaining to his son, and as usual, she had to make it about her. Money wondered what even attracted him to Brooklyn in the first place. It must have been her looks because her attitude was nasty as hell. He hadn't seen his son in months, and here her stupid ass wants to play games. The initial agreement was that their son would visit Brooklyn's aunt down south for the summer. The summer was long gone, and there were still no signs of Sincere. If Money could've taken back having a child by Brooklyn's trifling ass, then he certainly would have.

When Money had first started fucking with her, he had no idea that she already had three other kids. That alone would've made him run the other way. He had lost all respect for Brooklyn when he caught her upstairs in one of the rooms at the club engaged in a threesome with another stripper and some old head who was known for having paper. Brooklyn had her legs spread wide open like she was parting the Red Sea, getting her pussy ate while she took dude's dick to the back of her throat. Under different circumstances, the girl on girl action would've turned Money on, but the site of his supposed to be girl turning tricks disgusted him. To make matters worse, Brooklyn didn't even attempt to stop what she was doing. She looked directly at Money and continued sucking away. From that day on Money treated her like the slut she portrayed herself to be.

"This here is about my son, not Destiny, so let's clear that up. And you will respect her in my presence." Money was trying his hardest not to cause a scene in public, but he would smack her brains loose if she didn't start providing some answers about his seed.

Brooklyn totally disregarded everything Money had just said. Whenever she saw Destiny, she went into attack mode. She would throw slur after slur until Destiny would respond.

"Ya bitch on mute tonight. That last ass whipping I put on her ass finally shut her up I see."

Destiny wanted so badly to jump out of the car and spit in Brooklyn's face. She despised the ground she walked on. Everything about Brooklyn screamed ratchet to the fourth degree. The only reason she could picture Money dealing with someone of her nature was due to having good coochie. Instead of reacting she moved to the driver's seat with her foot on the gas pedal. She was prepared to run her ass straight the fuck over!

Destiny was proud of how Money was handling the situation. Normally by now, he would've gone the fuck off. Money's son meant everything to him, and to him, Brooklyn was failing tremendously at being a mother. If she didn't get her shit together and quick, then the next step was filing to have full custody of their son. Money knew if he went now, he would have no problem showing the courts that Sincere wasn't in a stable environment. Especially since he had found access to Brooklyn's medical records, concerning her drug overdose. He was trying to give her the benefit of the doubt. Brooklyn was making it real clear by the way she was acting that she was too unfit to care for their child. Seeing one too many spectators forming a crowd, Money decided to leave before things got out of hand, but not before leaving Brooklyn a little warning.

"You got until the end of this month to have Sincere back home or you'll be seeing me in court."

"So, you mean to tell me, you going to take my son away from me?"

"Bitch please, you don't even have him now. Ya stupid ass out here shaking ya ass in the damn strip club. Now tell me how that would look in front of a judge? Brooklyn was so embarrassed, she couldn't say one single word in return, but Money was far from finished. "Cat got ya tongue, huh? All that fucking mouth you got and now ya ass is quiet."

"Nigga, fuck you!" Brooklyn shouted.

"No bitch, fuck you! The worst mistake I could've ever made in life was fucking you. You'll never get a chance to fuck with me again. Now get ya ass out of here, and go home."

Destiny sat back watching everything unfold. Brooklyn was finally getting a dose of her own medicine, and she loved every minute of it.

"Come on babe, let's go," Destiny said to Money. She was trying to have some nice alone time with her man. Her mother was keeping London for the next few days, and she wanted some rest. Between being a first-time mom, and trying to run the law firm, it was impossible for them to even get a few minutes together.

"Yeah, I think it's best for you to listen to ya bitch and go." Money stood so close to Brooklyn's face she could smell the scent of peppermint Lifesaver on his breath.

"Bitch, don't tempt me to smack fire from ya ass. You got three weeks to have my son back."

"Money, don't forget what type of scandalous bitch you're fucking with. I'll make your life a living hell if you think you're getting custody of Sincere. I'll be damned if you and the next bitch play house with my son," Brooklyn said pissed off. Money had certainly made her shit list for the year, and his name was now at the top.

"Don't play with me Brooklyn," Money said through clenched teeth.

"Nigga, this ain't a game. If you think I'm playing, try me. Now as far as I'm concerned, this conversation is now officially over. Now move this piece of shit out of my way so I can leave. I got business to tend to." Destiny backed the car up enough so Brooklyn could get out.

"Destiny, are you ready for your first client?" She didn't have a clue as to what Money was talking about. She remained quiet as she waited for him to elaborate.

"Have my bail money ready at any time. Brooklyn's ass is up to some sheisty shit. You never underestimate what that bitch is capable of doing."

"Say no more. I got ya back boo."

*****

Brooklyn was late as hell arriving at Sharnese's house, but she didn't care. Brooklyn took a minute to look around the quiet neighborhood. There was no mistaking this area for the projects. Sharnese had moved on up like George and Weezy Jefferson. She got out of the car and rang the doorbell. Murda answered the door

Bridgette I'esha

wearing just a wife beater and some red Jordan basketball shorts. Brooklyn licked her lips seductively and said

"Hey Murda. How are you doing? You are looking fine mighty fine." There was no shame in nothing she did. Here she was standing in her cousin's house flirting with her man like it was acceptable. *My cousin's man or not he can definitely get the business. I just might have to add him to my to fuck list. Yeah, I'm a do just that.* Brooklyn's leg swiped Murda's crotch trying to get a quick feel of what he was working with between his legs.

"Aye Nese, ya cousin, is here," Murda said. He was feeling uncomfortable being alone with Brooklyn. *This thot ass bitch is really trying to feel my dick and shit while my girl right in the other room. I don't know what type of games this bitch playing.*

Murda left Brooklyn standing right where she was while he went into the living room and joined Sharnese on the sofa. When Brooklyn walked in she saw Sharnese sitting looking pretty. Good genes ran in their family.

"Well, I'm not going to hold up you two lovebirds, so I'll just get straight to business. Does the name "Kas" ring a bell to either one of you?" Brooklyn asked while studying the faces of both Sharnese and Murda. The entire atmosphere changed in the room as both Sharnese and Murda thought about their last encounter with that nigga Kas. Murda wasted no time pulling out his .45 and aiming it at Brooklyn's head. He didn't trust anything about her. From the moment she walked through the door, he could tell she wasn't shit.

"You better start talking and start talking now," Murda said with saliva flying everywhere. Just that quick he had transformed. When he got like that, there wasn't anything anybody could say to calm him down.

"Can you put the gun away?" Brooklyn said in a nervous tone.

"Not until I get some answers. You might as well get to talking," Murda said with his .45 now pressed against Brooklyn's temple.

"Well, some nigga named Kas stopped me when I was coming from out of the club. He told me he needed help finding his brother. When he showed me a picture of you, I told him I knew who you were. Then he offered me fifty grand to help me take you out." Brooklyn made sure to leave out the part about her talking shit about Sharnese. She was trying to make herself seem as innocent as possible.

"Is that all you said?" Murda questioned Brooklyn. Something about her story wasn't adding up to him.

"Yeah, that was it."

"Well, you can get yo shit, and get ya ass out of my house then." Murda grabbed Brooklyn by her arm and shoved her towards the door. He was on the verge of filling her body up with bullet holes.

Brooklyn didn't even put up an argument as she snatched up her purse. "Nese. I'll call you in the morning." Brooklyn saw herself to the door making sure to put a switch in her hips. Once Murda heard the door close, he started in on Sharnese.

"I don't want you nowhere near ya cousin! That girl is nothing, but bad news."

"But babe!"

"Sharnese, I'm serious. Ya cousin is going to wind up getting you hurt. With that stunt, she's put our lives in even more danger. From here on out you will have a bodyguard around the clock escorting you everywhere you need to go. As long as this nigga is still around I can't risk leaving you alone. I wouldn't be able to live with myself if something was to happen to you or our unborn child. In a couple of days, Money and I will have to take a business trip for a few days. I'll make arrangements for you to stay with Destiny while I'm away."

Sharnese sucked her teeth and rolled her eyes. She hated when Murda treated her like a child. At times, he was a little overprotective, but she knew it was for her own good. The fact that she was going to have someone looking over her shoulder every five minutes was going to take some getting used to. Sharnese liked coming and going as she pleased. With her being pregnant, she knew she wouldn't be able to properly defend herself if somebody came at her the wrong way.

"Murda, I'm a grown ass woman who's very capable of taking care of herself. I don't need a damn babysitter keeping tabs on me. What he gon do, come in the bathroom and wipe my ass for me after I shit too?" Sharnese asked being a smart ass.

Not in the joking mood, Murda ignored Sharnese's smart remark. He knew Sharnese was independent. She had made that very clear the first day they had met. She didn't need a man for anything, but she deserved one to treat her like the queen she was. It was a good thing Murda wasn't a weak man, or else he wouldn't have known what to do with a strong woman like Sharnese.

"What about when I go to work at the shop, will he be there too?"

"Yes Sharnese, and it's not up for discussion. Ben will be here first thing in the morning, so you two can get aquatinted with one another. Now, I'm going to bed. You're more than welcome to join me if you'd like," Murda said trying to sound so proper. He knew his ass was certified hood.

"I'll be up there in a few, I need some time to myself to think."

"Suit ya self." He gave her a smack on her butt before walking up the stairs.

An hour later, Murda rolled over to an empty space in the bed. Sharnese wasn't there. Immediately he went into panic mode. He raced downstairs and found her cuddled up on the sofa, eating popcorn and watching Tyler Perry's television show *The Haves and the Have Not's*. She was tuned in so hard she never even heard Murda come down. She was at the part where Veronica had just told her son Jeffrey that Melissa was pregnant with his child. It was clear as day that the boy was gay, yet she kept pressuring him to be with a woman. You know how some parents are when it comes to their children. They're just in denial about some things.

"Come on to bed Nese," Murda said.

She jumped at the sound of his voice causing her to drop all her popcorn on the floor. She looked at him and rolled her eyes. The popcorn and Murda would have to wait until her show went off. There were only a few more minutes left, and she wasn't about to miss it. Murda was just about to spark his blunt up when he remembered the doctor mentioning that second-hand smoke was more harmful to a person than smoking it themselves.

The show had finally ended. Sharnese couldn't believe that Veronica's ass had set the house on fire while her husband slept. That bitch was crazy for real. Sharnese didn't care much for Veronica anyway. She was team Candace all the way. She made her way to the staircase cutting off all the lights in the process.

"Are you gonna sit there in the dark or are you going to join me in bed?" Sharnese said mocking Murda from just a few minutes ago. He wasted no time following her up the stairs.

Chapter Five

Brooklyn sat home in her kitchen downing a coke and Hennessey while she thought about how Money had clowned her in front of everybody. The brown liquor wasn't doing anything, but making her madder by the second. Out of nowhere, she began hitting herself in the face with the shot glass. She continued to do this until the glass broke. Blood trickled down her face, but she didn't stop there. She searched through all the cabinets until she found the object she was looking for. She came across some thick rope and placed it around her neck. Brooklyn pulled the rope so tight she could feel her airway being cut off. Being that her complexion was so light, it didn't take long for her skin to bruise. She threw dishes all over the entire floor and ran her head into the wall. When she saw the damage she had done, she picked up the cordless phone and dialed 911.

"911, what's the emergency?" The dispatcher asked.

"My child's father Sincere Williams physically assaulted me," Brooklyn said fake crying into the phone. She picked up more dishes and threw them around the kitchen just to add some sound effects. "Ma'am please hurry and send someone over here! He's going to kill me!"

"What's your location miss?"

"I'm at 6496 Continental Drive, please hurry."

"Someone is on the way."

That was all Brooklyn needed to hear before she hung up the phone. A huge smile spreads across her face. "I told you not to fuck with me Money."

When the officers arrived, they asked her if she wanted to press charges, and of course, she said yes. Brooklyn was then escorted to the precinct to fill out the necessary paperwork. After everything was completed, she was ensured that a warrant would be placed for Money's arrest.

Brooklyn walked out of the police station a very happy woman. She didn't have not one ounce of remorse in her soul. She could've easily left the situation alone, but she felt that Money needed to be taught a lesson. She knew she wasn't the perfect mother

Bridgette I'esha

figure, but she truly did love her children. Having them at such a young age, introduced her to some things her mind wasn't ready to process.

While all her friends were in high school getting ready for prom and graduation she was working at a strip club trying to take care of a child when she was still a child herself. With no guidance and no one to look up to, she did the best she could. It was her lack of knowledge about abstinence that she ended up with four kids by the time she had turned 23. Out of all her baby daddies, Money was the only one who took care of his kid. Most fathers just paid child support and cared less if they ever saw their child. Money played a big role in Sincere's life. Doctor's appointments, holiday's, daycare, etc. He was always there. He made sure their son didn't want for anything. It wasn't even about the material things. He actually spent time with him.

Now he was being charged with one count of aggravated assault, and one count of aggravated battery. Brooklyn couldn't wait to see the look on Money's face when they went to arrest his dumb ass. Out of all people, he should've known Brooklyn didn't play fair. She just wanted Money to herself. The fact that he was with Destiny left a nasty taste in her mouth. He had made it clear on numerous occasions that the two of them would never happen again. If only she had done right in the beginning, then she would not have been going through this shit now. Anybody else would have called Brooklyn a scorned baby mama, but she had no reason to be bitter. Money had once given her the opportunity to be his, but she fucked it up by tricking. When Brooklyn finally got home, she made sure all her doors were locked before taking it down for the night.

*****

Kas sat in his boxed Chevy Caprice staring at Murda's two-story home. He had paid Brooklyn twenty of the fifty grand he'd promised for providing information pertaining to Murda's location. It didn't take long for him to start firing shots.

BLAT! BLAT! BLAT! The glass window in Murda and Sharnese's bedroom shattered into a million pieces. Quick with his hands, Murda pushed Sharnese onto the floor.

"Nese get underneath the bed now and don't move until I say so." She did as she was told fearing for her life. Murda was able to retrieve his gun from the nightstand. Murda fired back, blasting off shot after shot. With his sniper vision, he let another shot off. This one barely missed Kas's head. He managed to shoot the driver's window out. Murda continued to fire shots until the chamber was empty. Kas struggled to start the ignition. It wouldn't turn over.

POW! POW! POW! Murda loaded more ammunition inside his .45. This time he shot out one of the back tires. He was trying to make it so Kas wouldn't make it home tonight. Murda contemplated going outside and putting a permanent hole in Kas's head, but he was too afraid to leave Sharnese alone. On the last turn, Kas was finally able to get the car running. He put his foot on the pedal and sped up out of there, but not before Murda let off another shot. Once he was sure Kas was out of sight he ran to make sure Sharnese was alright.

"Nese, you good?" Murda asked concerned about her well-being.

"A little shaken up, but other than that, I'm good."

He was relieved to hear her say those words. "Pack some clothes for a while. I got to get you away from here. You may not want to hear this, but I believe your cousin set us up," Murda said making accusations against Brooklyn. In the streets, it was always innocent until proven guilty, but Murda didn't give a damn about any of that. In his eyes, the bitch was guilty, plain and simple. God couldn't even tell him otherwise. Sharnese didn't want to believe that Brooklyn would be so cruddy, but all the signs pointed to her. Very few people knew where they rested their heads, and it was kind of funny how shots were fired right after she left. Murda knew if he didn't dead the issue soon, then it would only escalate into something bigger.

"Aye Nese, you straight?" He called out, hoping she was packed and ready to roll. Murda had called Ben while Sharnese was getting her things together. When Murda called and told him he needed his services, Ben slid out of the warm twat he was laid up in. Whenever Murda needed him, he dropped everything he was doing to come to his aid. Ben had been down with Murda and his crew for a very long time. He was pretty much considered to be family. Not only was he Murda's godfather he was also Big Jimmy's former business partner and right-hand. Way back when Murda was a young boy he had always seen his interest in the street life. Out of concern, Ben expressed his opinion to Jimmy, and surprisingly he gave him his blessings. On Murda's sixteenth birthday, Ben presented him with his first kilo. Now, Murda didn't know a damn thing about distributing anybody's dope, but it damn sure didn't take

Bridgette I'esha

him long to learn and master the trade. His strategy was simple, keeping the customers happy. Once he let a local dope fiend sample some of his uncut product word began buzzing around town. All the old dope heads wanted some of the "fish" he was slanging. The main reason everyone one loved him was that he was always so generous. Anything he sold, he made sure the amount was always over and for that alone, he never lost a customer. From there he linked up with Money, and they'd been on ever since. Murda's phone went off. It was Ben letting him know he was outside.

"Aye Nese," he called out again. Not getting a fast-enough response, he barged into the bathroom and found her doubled over in pain. She was holding her stomach real tight as she rocked back and forth.

"What's wrong?" He asked.

"Nothing major. These Braxton Hicks have been kicking my ass lately."

Murda squished up his face. He had no clue as to what Sharnese was talking about. She saw the expression he had on his face and rolled her eyes.

Bridgette I'esha

"Do you listen to anything the doctor be saying?" She asked tapping her feet on the bathroom tile waiting for an answer.

"Not really. I leave all that shit to you. Just let me know when my prince is ready to make his grand entrance."

Sharnese laughed as the pain increased. Murda always did a good job keeping a smile on her face when they were on good terms. One thing about their relationship, when they were good, they were really good! There were plenty of bitches who would have killed to be in her position, and she knew that. Sharnese saw the envious stares she got from other females when they were together in public, but she paid those bitches no mind. If she worried about them, then she would become one of them. Another worried bitch. The attention she got from them only made her step her game up even harder. A queen never comes off her throne to address a peasant, and that's how she preferred to keep it. It only made her want to love Murda even more.

Murda smiled at Sharnese. Even with sweatpants and no make-up on, she was still gorgeous. Even though he'd fucked up months ago, he never once worried about her fucking around with another nigga. She never had a problem letting a nigga know that she was his backbone. He could have left Sharnese alone in a room with twenty butt naked men with big Mandingo dicks flying everywhere, and he wouldn't have a thing to worry about.

"I'm ready. Just take my luggage downstairs for me."

Murda grabbed her bags and shouted out, "God damn. What you got inside here a damn body?"

"Fuck around again, and it will be your body," she said with a crazed look on her face before she fell out laughing. "I got to be prepared. I don't know how long you plan on having me cooped up in a damn hotel." She pulled the remaining luggage downstairs. Murda introduced Ben and Sharnese to one another.

"Hi, I'm Sharnese. How are you doing this time of morning?" She asked politely. It was well after three-thirty in the morning. She just wanted Murda to hurry up, and get her checked into a hotel so that she could get some sleep.

"The name is Benny." He took her hand and kissed it slightly. Sharnese snatched her hand back in an instant. She wasn't used to another man beside Murda doing such things. Not sure of what to say, she just smiled in return. Ben saw how uncomfortable she was and apologized.

"I'm sorry. I didn't mean any harm at all. Your beauty is just so remarkable." He hoped Sharnese would forgive him. He wouldn't dare risk his life by betraying Murda. He knew Murda had no picks when he came to who he would take out. Murda would shoot your grandmother while she was cooking Sunday dinner if it meant getting his point across. His temper was uncontrollable, and anyone who crossed his path was asking for trouble.

"You're fine. You just caught me off guard with that one," Sharnese said in a jokingly matter.

Ben kept his eyes locked on her the entire time. The attraction he had towards her was very strong. He imagined bending her over on the carpeted stairway while she threw her ass in several circles. The tight sweatpants she wore left him little to wonder about. He could see the fine print of her fat pussy. The split separating both of her lips had him wanting to taste it right there. Ben felt the pre-cum spill from the tip of his dick. He moved from side to side trying to stop himself from exploding in front of her.

"Yo Ben, you good?" Murda said watching him bounce around.

"Yeah man, I'm good."

Bridgette I'esha

"You sure? It looks like you got to piss or some shit of that nature. I mean if you got to use the bathroom it's right down the hall."

"Can we go already? I am very pregnant and tired," Sharnese said interrupting their conversation. Murda knew Sharnese could get agitated when she was deprived of sleep.

"The Queen is becoming impatient," Murda said being sarcastic. Let's get her to a room."

His phone vibrated as they were on their way out the door. "What it be?" He said answering the blocked call. For a few seconds, the line remained silent. "Yo who the fuck is this?" He asked again. Still no answer only heavy breathing could be heard. Murda pressed the end button on the phone. He didn't have the time to be playing games with the unknown caller. His night had been exhausting enough. He saw Sharnese cutting her eyes over at him. *Man, here we go with this shit. A nigga can't win for losing around here.* "Go head Nese," he said before she could get any words out.

Sharnese wasn't having it though. Snapping her neck, she did a full three-sixty around the sidewalk. Murda knew he had fucked up that time. Sharnese put up with a lot of stuff, but telling her to go ahead before she got started was a definite no-no.

"Go head my ass. Who was that on the phone?" She questioned with her face tore up. She had only reacted like that to see if he would tell the truth about who was on the phone. She didn't even give him time to process his thoughts before she went in on him again. "Um, hello. I am talking to you." Her attitude was on high. Just thinking about him touching another woman made her blood boil. She didn't care if it happened while they were on a break. There was another woman walking who could proudly say that she'd had her man. It was bad enough that he cheated in the first place, and here they were dealing with a stalking chick. She tapped her foot on the hard cement while she waited for an answer.

Murda said a silent prayer hoping things didn't turn left. "I don't know, probably that silly girl playing on my jack again, but don't worry your pretty little self about it." On the inside, Sharnese was smiling from ear to ear, but she wasn't about to let him know it. She kept her mean mug on and walked off. Ben opened the doors to Murda's black on black Range Rover and made sure they were both secured properly before peeling off out of the driveway.

Bridgette I'esha

The first few minutes of the ride was quiet. Nobody said anything as everyone was lost deep in their thoughts. The whole Kas bullshit was stressing Murda out. It was the second time in a few months that his life could've been taken from him. The more he thought about it, the colder his heart grew. It was time to put a stop to it once and for all. He looked over at Sharnese, who was sleeping peacefully. Murda blamed himself for putting her in these fucked up situations. Had he not introduced her to this life, she would've never become a walking target. Murda's name was well-known in the streets of Brooklyn. Everyone knew his murder game was vicious, but lately, he had been caught slipping one too many times. Time wasn't on his side. It was either get focused and body Kas or become another victim on the *First 48*.

The car had finally come to a stop. They had arrived at their destination. The lights in the city was always a beautiful view at night. Murda got out of the car and went inside the hotel to check in. He didn't bother waking up Sharnese until everything was squared away.

Once they reached their suite, Sharnese wasted no time peeling off each layer of clothing she had on. She hurried to the bathroom to take a shower. Once the steaming hot water hit her skin, she immediately woke up. She lathered her bath pouf with Mango Temptation shower gel by Victoria's Secrets making sure to clean every part of her body. The shower was where she found her peace of mind. As the water penetrated her skin, she thought about the place she was at in life. It seemed like every area was going good, except the part that included Murda. If it wasn't one thing, then it was another. The drama was constant in their lives. Between the side chicks, and his beef in the streets, she didn't know how she was holding herself together. Yeah, Murda had told her he would handle the Natalie issue, but that was something she felt like she had to take care of herself. It was taking him forever and a day to seek revenge on Kas. She rinsed off the suds, turned the water off and stepped out of the tub. Careful not to slip on the floor as she dried off, she looked at her body in the mirror. Not a stretch mark was in sight as her belly continued to expand. Putting lotion on her body, she brushed her teeth and walked into the bedroom with no clothes on hoping Murda didn't want to have sex. Luckily for her when she approached the bed he was already rolled over fast asleep. When she went to go lay on the bed, she felt like she was in paradise. It was so

Bridgette I'esha

soft and comfortable. The sheets melted against her body. This was how every Queen was supposed to sleep. After finding a comfortable sleeping position, she joined her love and fell asleep right beside him.

*****

Destiny was in her office going over the details of a potential client's case when she heard continuous knocking at her front door. She grabbed her red silk robe from the couch and proceeded to the front door. The officers didn't give her a chance to ask any questions before shoving an arrest warrant in her face.

"Where is Sincere Williams?" The officer said in a very unprofessional manner. Destiny was trying her hardest to remain calm, but the fact that the officer was so rude made it hard.

"What is this about?" She asked hoping to get to the bottom of it all.

"We ask all the questions here," the white cop named Sam said as he spits on the steps barely missing her feet.

Destiny looked at him with pure hate in her eyes. If it weren't for all the police brutality on minorities going on, she most definitely would've snapped. She wasn't trying to become a victim of something so senseless. The black cop named Rudy saw the tension building between the two and decided to intervene.

"Ma'am, it's for the assault and battery of a Brooklyn Santana," he said handing her the warrant to read for herself.

"You got to be fucking kidding me," Destiny said as she read the warrant. This only made her regret not whooping Brooklyn's ass the night before. In her mind, she counted to three to cool off. *As soon as their asses leave I'ma need me a fat ass blunt of loud, and a glass of red wine. This shit is too much to take in at one time.* She hadn't smoked in months, so it was well overdue. Handing the warrant back, she hollered Money's full name loud and clear. "Sincere Williams get in here now!"

When Money heard his name being called he got up to see what the ruckus was all about. Wearing only some boxers he was greeted at the door with Destiny and the two officers. "Are you Sincere Williams?" The officer asked with the handcuffs held high up in the air.

"Yeah, why?" He replied really confused.

"Turn around and place your hands behind your back." Officer Sam placed the cuffs on Money's wrist extra tight. Money was sure the metal would cut into his skin. "You're under arrest for the assault and battery against a Brooklyn Santana," the cop said. He then went ahead and read Money his Miranda Rights.

"Meet me down at the station," Money said to Destiny as he was placed in the back seat of the patrol car, and hauled away.

Destiny ran into the house and viewed the surveillance cameras they had outside the house. Money had gotten them installed just in case someone tried to burglarize their home while they were away on vacation. Sure enough, the video showed that Money was indeed home with her the entire time. She made two extra copies of the video. She placed one in her briefcase while locking the other in a safe spot. Brushing her hair into a tight, neat bun. She threw on a black pencil skirt and a pink blouse. Before placing her feet into a pair of black pumps. Her outfit was plain and simple, but she wasn't expecting to make a visit to the precinct either.

*****

Money was interrogated for hours before they went ahead and booked him. It was the weekend, so no Judge would be able to see him until Monday morning. After speaking with Destiny, he was more than certain that everything would work out in his favor.

Bridgette I'esha

Money knew Brooklyn could be petty, but he didn't think she would take it this far. He tried to get some rest, but the cot that they called a bed was hard as rocks. It was impossible to get comfortable on that thing. The stench of piss made him want to gag from the smell. He was in a holding cell with three other men, who looked to be heavily intoxicated. He sat there praying that the next day would fly by.

Chapter Six

People all over town were talking about the big wedding Murda and Sharnese was planning. Kas smiled as he sat the invitation down on the brown coffee table. He had one of his jump-offs getting her hair done by Sharnese on the regular, hoping to gather as much information as possible. He figured their wedding day would be the perfect day to take care of them both. The top of the invitation was even titled "Fairytales do end happily." *This is going to be a memory of a lifetime.* Kas said to himself.

The date was less than two months away. Kas wanted this to be his final attempt at ending Murda's life. He looked at the time. He was supposed to be meeting the connect to re-up on some Oxytocin. It was crazy how getting high off pills had become the new weed. It was like weed wasn't a strong enough high anymore. Kas smoked loud from time to time, but his drug of choice was the powdered stuff. He pulled out a crisp fifty-dollar bill and rolled it up. He sprinkled some cocaine onto his small glass tray and snorted a line. His nose burned a little as the effects of the coke kicked in. Kas sat back on the leather furniture stuck in a daze. Chanel appeared from one of the backrooms. He kept her around to feed his sexual appetite. She wasted no time getting on her knees to satisfy him. Not only did she enjoy putting her mouth to work. She loved the tips Kas always hit her off with. It only took her a couple of minutes to suck him completely dry. Before she could blink her eyes, he was busting off in her mouth. He threw a few Benjamin's on the floor beside her; before sending her on her way. He then went into the bathroom and washed up. He threw on his Navy-Blue Polo Shirt and some Khaki Shorts before making his way out the door.

*****

Kas sat in the food court of Manhattan's Mall waiting on Pierre the pill connect to arrive. He was over an hour late which was making Kas mad and nervous at the same time. He didn't know if Pierre had gotten knocked off or what. All he knew was time was money, and he was missing out on plenty of it. Another ten minutes passed before he finally decided to show up.

"Kaseem, my man," Pierre said with a wide grin on his face.

Bridgette I'esha

Kas looked at the shopping bags he was holding and was pissed. "You mean to tell me, you were out shopping while we're supposed to be conducting business?" Kas asked getting a little loud.

"No, no, this is all business, my friend. Sit down and let me explain." He pulled a chair out from underneath the table gesturing for him to have a seat. Kas did as he was told. Pierre looked around to see if anyone was watching them. Nothing was out of the ordinary. Kids were sitting down eating ice cream with their parents while the babies cried to be picked up. "In these bags are women's high heels," Kas said nothing as he let him explain. "Each pair of these heels contain your pills inside of the soles. Kas sat there smiling from ear to ear. That was something he would have never thought of. Nobody would ever suspect that they were trafficking pills inside of the shoes. "All you have to do is carefully cut out the sole, and the rest is history."

Kas had to admit he was slightly impressed. He gladly took the bags from out of Pierre's hands. It was time for him to make up for his losses. After exchanging cash for product, Kas was on his way to bag up some of the pills.

Jermaine and Kas were putting the pills into bottles to be distributed in the streets. Business stayed booming for them. "Any news on this Murda cat?" Jermaine asked eagerly. Lately, there had been no noise being made.

"None except for this wedding their planning," Kas replied.

"I say we blow that bitch up!" Jermaine said getting excited.

"Relax cuz, I'm already ten steps ahead of you. I don't care who gets hurt in the process. The only thing I'm concerned about is blowing this nigga's head off his shoulders," Kas said as he placed the last of the pills inside a dark green bottle.

Kas had a few regular customers who bought pills daily. His main girl Nina worked as a pharmacist in one of the local hospitals. It was nothing for him to get labels with his client's names on them. It was a little past six, and like clockwork, there was a knock at the door. Kas took the safety off his gun and peeked out of the blinds. Outside stood Mikey. He was one of Kas's favorite, faithful customers. Mikey was once at the top of his class in college. After being injured in a bad car collision, he suffered severe back pain. The pills he had been prescribed helped ease the pain, but as the days progressed his body became dependent on them. After a while, he lost everything. His full scholarship was revoked, and his family disowned him. Now at age thirty-four, he was nothing more than a pill-popping petty hustler. Any type of hustle he could get, he was on it. Kas opened the door and let him in.

"What's crackin'?" Kas asked Mikey as he watched him fidget around with his hands.

"I can't call it. Trying to get rid of this here back pain if you know what I mean," he said handing Kas a crisp hundred-dollar bill.

Jermaine took out two pills and placed them in Mikey's hand. The only reason he got them for a deal was because they knew he would be back to spend some of that U.S. Currency he had left in his pocket.

"I'll get up with you later. I'm about to slide through them other spots before I head on in," Kas said.

"Alight, cuz." Jermaine let Kas see himself out as he waited for a few more customers.

*****

Money was in the holding cell when he saw a familiar face walk by. "Nah, it can't be." He mumbled to himself as he walked to the cell's door to get a closer look. Sure enough, it was Natalie, better known as Detective O'Neal to the precinct. She just so happened to be there for a meeting with the Captain to discuss the case they were building on Murda.

"Yo, my man," Money said to the older man sitting next to him.

"What's up young blood?" The old man responded.

"Do you know anything about the broad that just walked passed here?"

"You must be talking about the undercover, Detective Natalie." Money had to make sure he was hearing things right, so he asked again.

"Did you just say, Detective?"

"Yeah, she's been setting all the dope boys up, and taking them down. As fine as she is who would ever expect for her to be the law?" The older man had been in and out of jail his entire life, so he had seen it all. He knew just about every officer who worked in the precinct on a first name basis.

Money thanked the man again. "Good looking man," and then went and sat down to think.

"No, problem." The old man said in return as he went back to reading his Daily Bread.

I can't believe this shit. Murda done jeopardized everything we've accomplished over some pussy. Who just so happens to be an undercover detective.

Money's mind was racing a thousand miles an hour. He didn't know how Murda was going to clean this mess up. It wasn't long before his thoughts were interrupted.

"Williams." The guard called out. "You're free to go." It was like music to his ears when Money heard his name being called to be released.

Outside, Destiny was impatiently waiting for Money to come out. With the videotape, she had, showing Money was at home at the time the assault took place they had no choice but to let her client free. She had been a nervous wreck the entire time. Over the weekend, she had barely gotten three hours of sleep. She was too busy worrying about Money's well-being. She ran her hands alongside her blouse trying to straighten out some of the wrinkles it possessed. The bags under her eyes made her look more hungover than tired. Once she got home, it would be all work and no play. So, sleep was out of the question.

Money being in jail made her despise Brooklyn even more. It was bitches like her who made it hard on women who were trying to go places in life. She had made a vow to leave the drama alone once she had London, but it seemed as though the streets were calling her name to make a return. Destiny had thought about just blowing her brains loose, but erased the thought when she thought about little Sincere. She had a soft spot in her heart when it came to him. Biologically he may not have been her child, but with the love, she gave him you couldn't tell her otherwise. For the time being, she was going to leave the situation alone. Revenge was best served on a cold plate.

Money emerged from the jail a happy man. He couldn't understand how so many men got out and went right back. Having someone yelling in his face, telling him what to do wasn't something he could tolerate. His body reeked of sweat and musk. He had refused to shower in front of a bunch of faggots who couldn't wait to lust over his body and get a glimpse of his man. On top of that, he was starving. The mess they served as food, he wouldn't even feed it to a dog. The sunlight brought him back to reality. He appreciated the light that shined in his eyes. It reminded him that he was a free man.

Money barely acknowledged Destiny as he climbed into the front seat of their all white Cadillac Escalade. Destiny took his attitude as being pissed about going to jail, so she said nothing as they drove off. The distance Money was displaying was driving her crazy. Normally, they talked about everything. She didn't know what this new shit was, but she didn't care for it one bit. "Talk to me, babe. What's wrong?"

"Nothing," he replied dryly.

"So, we lying now? That's where we at?" She asked smacking him upside his head. "I thought we were better than that."

"Destiny right now is not the time for the dumb shit," he said lighting his Black Cherry Flavored Black and Mild. He inhaled the smoke and relaxed a bit. "We got a bigger problem on our hands."

"Bae, what's going on?" She asked having a difficult time keeping her eyes on the road.

"The bitch from the hospital is not only a realtor but the fucking law also," Money said as the truck swerved off the road, barely missing a light pole in the process. That was the last thing she was expecting to hear him say. All the action gave Destiny a headache.

"Does Murda and Nese know about this?" She asked.

Money looked at her like she had just asked the dumbest question ever. "Do you think he would've fuck with her if he knew she was the police?"

Destiny sat there wondering why she had asked in the first place. Already tired, hearing this made her want to say the hell with work and crawl straight into their California King sized bed once they got home. "We'll deal with all of this tomorrow. Right now, let's just go home, and get some rest." She put the car in drive, praying they would get home safely.

Chapter Seven

Sharnese and Destiny were in the middle of the floor at Destiny's house going over the final details for the wedding. The colors, of course, were dark red, white and just a tad bit of silver. She didn't have a set budget as she wanted this to be her first and last marriage. Once her and Murda said their vows at the altar, divorce would not be an option. The wedding was quickly approaching, and Sharnese was running herself crazy. She was thirty-six weeks along, and all she kept thinking about was what if she went into labor before then. Destiny had been a big help with the planning. Anytime she saw Sharnese getting overwhelmed, she gladly took over. The girls didn't mind each other's company. It gave them time to catch up with each other about a few things.

"How are things going at the law firm?" Sharnese said stuffing her mouth with a handful of grapes. During her pregnancy, she made sure to maintain a healthy diet. She wasn't trying to gain a bunch of unnecessary weight which she couldn't get off afterward. It was bad enough her nose had spread halfway across her face.

"Stressful as hell. When people from the hood heard I owned my own firm, the cases started piling in out of nowhere. But so far, it's not too bad."

"That's what's up. I'm proud of you. You've really come a long way. Besides we need someone to defend the dope boy's in our life."

"You're right about that. Money mentioned something about a big announcement that he and Murda plan on making. I wonder what that could be about," Destiny said as she counted the guest list one last time. Sharnese had specifically said no more than one thousand guests, but every time she turned around Murda was steady inviting people. With the beef with Kas still going on, they had decided to make it an invitation access only. Meaning if you didn't have it in your hand at the door, then you would not be getting inside.

"Girl, I couldn't tell you. To be honest, I've barely said two words to Murda since this shit about the bitch Natalie being an undercover detective came to light," Sharnese said wiping a few tears from her face. "Don't get me wrong, I love Murda with all my heart, but it's like there's always something trying to make us fail as a couple. A lot of the time I find myself questioning if I'm ready to fully commit myself to this lifestyle. Shit, this ain't easy." Sharnese laughed.

She needed someone to vent to. So much had happened over the last year, she didn't know who she was anymore. How she went from being a naïve girl to the first lady to a dope boy, she would never understand. Love really makes you do some crazy things. She couldn't deny the fact that besides Murda's cheating ways he was a damn good man. He provided without her having to ask. Although she had her own coins and plenty of them. He always told her to stack her money. As long as they were on the same page, then anything was possible for them to overcome.

Destiny grabbed a few napkins from out of the kitchen and handed them to Sharnese. She could feel the pain in her best friend's words as she spoke. For as long as she could remember Sharnese was never one to be emotional. She always kept everything bottled up inside. Destiny felt exactly where she was coming from. Her and Money's relationship was far from perfect. She might not have had to deal with the drama from the side chicks, but dealing with

Brooklyn's ass was more than enough. There were times when she wanted to throw in the towel, and call it quits, but she had never been one to give another bitch what they wanted. She would ride with her man until the wheels fell off, or kill him herself before she gave another female the satisfaction of thinking they made her give up.

"Honey, it comes with the territory. It took me a long time to get used to this. After dealing with the drama your cousin constantly brings our way, we can conquer anything. If you love that man as much as you claim, then make it work. You aren't going to find a relationship in this world that doesn't have problems." That was all Destiny had to say on the matter. At the end of the day, her opinion didn't matter because she wasn't the one who had to sleep with him every night. Sharnese felt much better after getting how she felt off her chest.

"Look at my ass up here crying. I'll be glad when this baby decides to drop. I'm sick of crying about every little thing."

Destiny smiled at her best friend. She was glad to see her back in good spirits. "What else do we need to go over?" Destiny asked.

Bridgette I'esha

"That should be it. Sometime next week, we need to gather all the girls together to do one last dress fitting. I want everything to be finalized by then, so I can use the rest of this time to get some rest."

"Okay, do you have the baby's nursery set up?" Destiny asked changing the subject.

Sharnese put her head down in embarrassment and said, "With everything that's been going on, I haven't had time to even focus on the baby."

"Let me pour me a glass of wine. If I would have known that, it would've been finished a long time ago. You know what don't worry about it, everything's on me."

Sharnese covered her mouth. "Are you sure?" She asked.

"Girl please, this is my first nephew we're talking about. You know I got to make sure he's good. Besides, that's what friends are for, right?"

"Thanks, boo. I really appreciate it."

"Don't mention it. Now let's hop online and do some shopping. Money left me his credit cards, and I'm ready to burn a hole in his pockets."

They browsed the internet for hours having some retail therapy. By the time they were done Sharnese had everything she had needed for the baby plus more. It was truly a blessing. The baby monitor sounded off alerting Destiny that London had awakened for her feeding. It was a good thing she had breast milk pumped in the fridge. She had forgotten all about the glass of wine she had drunk. Destiny went to stand up, but Sharnese stopped her.

"Rest ya nerves, I got it," Sharnese said to her.

"I'm supposed to be helping you, and here you are giving me a break," she said propping her feet up on top of the ottoman in front of the couch.

"You good. Besides I need all the practice, I can get. You know I don't have a clue about being a mother."

"It comes naturally. You'll be fine."

Baby London's cries grew louder. Destiny got up and prepared the bottle while Sharnese went to get her out of the nursery. She patted the baby lightly on her back, and the crying ceased. Her maternal instinct had kicked in. Taking a seat in the brown rocking chair, she placed the pink Minnie Mouse blanket over the baby's back and rocked her back to sleep. Somewhere between singing several lullabies, she had rocked herself to sleep also. Destiny noticed it was taking Sharnese a long time to return. When she stepped into the nursery, she found both Sharnese and her princess out for the count. She carefully removed London from her arms and placed her back into the bassinet. She kissed her on the forehead, and quietly exited the room. She had a bottle of wine to finish along with some more shopping to do.

*****

Brooklyn was at Kas's house waiting for him to return. He had left Chanel there to keep her company. Brooklyn's nerves were jittery as hell. Being in Kas's house had her thinking someone would run into his spot at any minute. She was downstairs in the basement watching an old episode of "Scandal" when Chanel walked in with a blunt sparked in her hand and a bottle of Gin wearing extra short coochie cutter shorts.

"You want to hit this?" Chanel asked. She knew Kas wasn't coming back anytime soon, so they may as well get comfortable around each other.

"Hell yeah, I need some of that in my life."

Chanel inhaled the blunt and passed it over to Brooklyn. She took a few puffs of the blunt and was impressed. They definitely weren't smoking any dirt. The weed had her higher than a kite. That along with the two cups of gin had her feeling good. Brooklyn stood up to stretch her legs, and almost stumbled into the glass end table. Holding on to Chanel's leg she caught her balance. She glanced up and caught Chanel staring at her. "What? Do I have a spot on me or something?"

Chanel eyed Brooklyn's entire body and licked her red coated lips. "You got a fat pussy," she responded. It was no secret that Chanel was bisexual. Most of the time she preferred to be in a man's arms, but every now and then she yearned for a woman's touch.

Brooklyn didn't know if it was the weed or the alcohol that had her clit jumping. She removed the one-piece romper she had on and revealed her bald neatly shaven cat. She never bothered to wear any panties. She liked to be free. She spread her pussy lips wide giving Chanel a clear view of the pink that resided in between her lips. Chanel motioned for her to come closer. Brooklyn wasted no time climbing over her head and sitting on her face. Chanel held onto Brooklyn's ass cheeks as she ate away like it was her last supper. Brooklyn had experimented with girls before, but this right here was something different. The more Chanel sucked the wetter Brooklyn became.

"Yes! Eat this pussy!" Brooklyn hollered out in ecstasy. The slurping sounds from Chanel's mouth made Brooklyn grind even harder against her face. She raised up from off Chanel, needing a minute to catch her breath. Chanel wasn't having it though. She pushed Brooklyn flat on her back. Locking their legs together in a scissors position. Chanel pressed her clit directly on top of Brooklyn's clit and moved around in a circular motion. Brooklyn came for the fourth time. She had never had a man make her feel as good as Chanel did, and she had, had her share of men. Chanel could feel Brooklyn's clit swell up twice its size. She grinded down even harder as they both released their water fountains at the same time. Chanel removed her legs from around Brooklyn's and rubbed her clit until she squirted her juices all over the place. Gathering their clothes, they headed upstairs to freshen up. By the time Kas returned Brooklyn was in his recliner watching some reality show. The lights were off, so he assumed she was asleep. He turned the lamp on dim. Brooklyn popped her head up.

"I'm glad I wasn't sleeping. You coming in here cutting all these damn lights on," she snapped.

"Last time I checked, I paid the bills in here not you. Now get ya ass up. We got business to discuss," he said taking a seat on the opposite side of the living room.

"We can also discuss my next payment."

"Don't start that bullshit," Kas said looking at the invitation to Murda's wedding in his hand for the hundredth time.

"Bullshit my ass. I'm about my coins. Now run me my money," Brooklyn said with her hand held out. Kas counted off two grand and threw it at her. She picked it up and frowned her face up.

"What the fuck is this?"

"Ya payment. What you think it is? Either take that and be satisfied or don't get anything and look stupid. You won't be getting another dime from me until this job is done. Now can we get down to business? I don't have time to be playing games."

Brooklyn said nothing as she wore a dumb expression on her face. Had they met under different circumstances Kas would have

Bridgette I'esha

been the perfect nigga to tame her. Brooklyn was a hot bitch, and she needed someone hotter than fish grease to cool her off.

"Carry on," she said ready to go home.

"The plan is I'm going to come to the wedding as your guest. All I need for you to do is act yourself and don't draw a lot of attention to us," he said.

"Well, that may be a problem," she said scratching her long weave.

"And why is that?" Kas asked.

"Because everywhere I go I draw nothing, but attention." She stood up and spun around a few times. "I mean look at me. How could this beauty not capture any eyes?"

"You gonna have to tone it down that day. I swear I won't hesitate to put a bullet in between your eyes if you fuck this up."

"Is that all?" She asked growing tired of listening to his mouth. It was time for her to leave before her mouth messed around and got her into some trouble she couldn't get out of.

"Yeah, now leave." After Kas heard the door slam he rolled a blunt of Kush and anticipated the day when he would have control over the streets.

Bridgette I'esha

Chapter Eight

Murda was at the stove in the kitchen of one of his trap houses, cooking up nine ounces of that "Superfreak."

"You good in here bro?" Money asked stepping beside the stove. It had been a minute since him, and Murda had to put in any real work, but it was the first of the month, and the fiends were on the prowl.

"Yeah, my nigga, I'm straight." Murda was working the hell out of his wrist. The magic he could produce with that, it was no wonder why they had raised to the top in no time.

"Alright, I'm ready to head back out on the block and make shit happen. Here, I almost forgot." Money handed Murda a knot of money wrapped in rubber bands.

"What's this?" Murda asked.

"All the money we've made in the last two hours."

Murda took the rubber band off and counted it out. It was only two in the morning, and already they had brought in over a ten-thousand-dollar profit. Murda hurried back over to the stove and put his wrist back to work. If the money was flowing like that, then he damn sure wasn't about to miss out on it. It was going to be a long night for them both. Sharnese was spending the night with Destiny, so he knew she was in good hands. Plus, he had Big Ben keeping a watch on the house. He had been told to shoot first and ask no questions if anything looked suspicious. Murda still had two birds to cook up before the morning traffic jam hit. He took a sip from his Red Bull hoping it would give him wings.

He focused hard on the task he was doing. He wasn't trying to fuck up a batch by being careless. It was a loss he couldn't afford to take. With the skills, he possessed in the kitchen it was impossible for him to mess up. He cooked up the remainder of the product in no time. By the time he was finished his wrist was literally on fire. The clock on the kitchen wall read five thirty. His body was beyond tired, but it was all a part of the lifestyle he chose. Unlike most niggas, he didn't hustle just to buy cars or to impress bitches. He did it to make sure his family was well taken care of if anything was to happen to

Bridgette I'esha

him. With the stash, he had saved up, and the money coming in from the real estate there was nothing in the world they would want for. At the age of twenty-seven, he had a twelve-year run in the game with no slip-ups until now. He didn't know what Natalie had up her sleeve, but he needed to find out before it was too late. He wanted to sit down and have a civilized conversation with her, but he knew Sharnese would kill him if he had any type of contact with her. He didn't need any more drama between the two of them. Their wedding day would be here soon, and he wasn't trying to do anything that would make her not become Mrs. Rodríguez.

*****

Murda and Money had a few hours left before they headed out of town for their last meeting with the connect. Everything had worked out for the best. They had already given their plug Romario a notice about them departing from the game for a little while. Romario was sad to hear about their departure. Murda and Money had brought him plenty of cash in their short time doing business together. Out of respect for them, he had agreed to give Pop a chance. He had only recalled meeting him once, but from what he did see, Pop was a man about his money, and that was a vibe he wanted to maintain. If he had felt otherwise, then Murda and Money would have been dead before they stepped foot off the Island.

Whenever Murda and Money came to the Island, they were always treated with great hospitality. Romario had a pool full of beautiful, exotic looking women. Each possessed features that you would only see in magazines. A Spanish band played inside the Sunroom, which was right next to the pool. Maria, the maid, had prepared an abundance of Caribbean cuisine.

"Welcome," Romario said greeting them both by the pool. He wanted to make their last business meeting more of a celebration.

"Is all of this for us?" Money asked, being the first one to speak up.

"Si, you and your partner have made me an even wealthier man. Without you two, my family back home wouldn't be able to live the lavish life that they now do."

Romario resided in Jamaica, but he was born and raised in Mexico. After leaving home at the age of twenty, he was given the opportunity to make some extra cash. What started off as him being the lookout for some local drug lords quickly turned him into being the head of an operation under his own organization. Ever since then he's been living in Jamaica, only visiting home on certain holidays.

"No disrespect, but can we get down to business? A nigga hasn't slept in days, and the smell of this food is only making my hunger pains stronger." They laughed at Murda's sense of humor, but he didn't find a thing funny. He was dead serious.

"Follow me this way," he said leading them down a dark corridor. Murda and Money exchanged looks of confusion. They had never taken this route to the mansion. The, further along, they walked the darker it became. The only light in the hall came from the candles burning on the wall. Finally, they had reached a room that more so portrayed a dungeon. The door swung open by itself. They took a few steps inside, and the door slammed shut behind them. Everything went black before them as the flames appeared in the old-fashioned fireplace. In front of the fireplace stood several canvases. Each separate one displayed pictures of their loved ones.

"What the fuck is going on Romario?" Murda asked. He was beyond pissed that he didn't have his tool on him. Romario's bodyguards had patted them down as soon as they arrived at the door.

Romario didn't permit any of his guests to enter inside of his home armed. He would be the only one making bodies drop in there.

"This is just a little insurance," he replied in return.

"Insurance on what?" Money chimed in.

"I need to be one hundred percent sure that your man in a thoroughbred," he said pointing to the picture of Pop. "I've had someone following your boy since we had last spoken. So far nothing has come up that would make me have to kill you both now."

Murda and Money understood exactly where he was coming from. They would have suspicions too if someone they hadn't known for too long, decided to hand over their throne to a youngin.

"Was this necessary?" Money asked.

"I found it was very necessary. I've worked too hard to let a hot head fuck it up. It's business and nothing personal. If I find that any loyalty has been broken by him, then one of your family members will die, a brutal, and gruesome death. No questions about it."

Murda's jaw tightened. He hated when threats were made. Money shot him a look while mouthing the words "Not here." He knew if Murda didn't calm down, they wouldn't return to the U.S. alive.

"In your suites, you both will find your final packages as well as a special farewell present from myself, of course. I'm sure you both will enjoy it. Cortez and Sincere, it has really been a pleasure doing business with the both of you." Romario left them to find their own way out. Money looked up at Murda, who was staring at the picture of Sharnese. The more he tried to exclude her from his lifestyle, the more he dragged her in.

"You good?" Money asked trying to remember the way to the backyard.

"Yeah!" He replied, finally looking away from the canvas. The blaze from the fire revealed the beads of sweat on his forehead.

"We'll be alright. We know Pop won't let us down. If we thought otherwise we wouldn't be passing all of this down to him."

"I hope you're right because I have no problem killing him myself. My family will not suffer due to someone else," Murda said no more as he walked out of the room to get squared away in his suite. He walked into the room and found a black duffel bag with his name written in large cursive print. He unzipped the bag and was amazed at how neatly the ten-thousand-dollar stacks were laid. He didn't bother to count it, as he estimated it to be about two hundred thousand dollars total.

*****

The next morning, Murda woke up with a vicious headache. He rolled over to find two naked women in the bed alongside him. The events of the night before were a total blur. He couldn't remember anything that had occurred the night before. He shook each of the girls until they woke up.

"I don't know who you are, but y'all got to get the hell out of my room."

The girls laid back down. After all the partying and fucking, they'd done the night before, they weren't trying to hear anything he had to say. Not being in the mood for any of the nonsense, Murda got up and went into the bathroom. He took a quick shower, making sure to wash off any scent that may have come from the two women. The last thing he wanted to do was bring Sharnese a disease home. He brushed his teeth and rinsed his mouth good with Listerine. He stared at his reflection in the mirror. He didn't even recognize the man before him.

Bridgette I'esha

Not getting any sleep was taking a toll on his body, and the stress from his beef in the streets didn't make it any better. Once he got home, he planned on spending as much time as he could with Sharnese. His conscious was eating at him, and he felt bad as hell for not being with her as much as he should have. He promised himself he would do better. He was ready to become someone's husband and here he was in bed with two females he didn't know. If he had caught Sharnese acting in such a way, he would have cut her loose. In just a couple of months, he would be twenty-eight years of age if he lived to see his birthday. He was at the point in life where he just wanted to settle down and explore the world. Murda wiped the dried-up toothpaste from around his mouth. He grabbed the duffel bag from off the floor and made his way down the flight of stairs in the hallway. When he reached, the last step Money was there waiting for him.

"You bout ready to roll?" Asked Money. His bags were already in his hands. Romario had a limo outside waiting to take them to the airport. Money was gulping down a rum and coke. No matter how many times he rode on an airplane, it still fucked with his head. He'd die first before he was forced to take another flight, he was ready to get home and put this business trip behind him. He still wasn't feeling the threats Romario had promised to deliver if Pop fucked up.

*****

Sharnese was in the middle of dying a client's hair Ruby Red when an unfamiliar female walked into the salon asking to speak to her.

"What can I do for you this morning?" The receptionist asked Natalie as she sat her purse on top of the counter.

"You can't do a thing for me," Natalie replied with much attitude.

"I'm looking for the bitch ass owner that goes by the name of Sharnese."

"Excuse me?"

"Sweetie, there's nothing to be excused about. Just tell Sharnese someone wants to speak to her."

Natalie was dead wrong for being rude to the receptionist, but she didn't care. Murda was still ignoring her phone calls which did nothing, but make her obsession with him even worse. If her calling him wasn't getting his attention, then she had to go to the

Bridgette I'esha

next best thing his prized possession, Sharnese. Renee got up from behind the desk and went to inform her boss of the trouble that awaited her out front.

"Excuse me, but um Sharnese you have a woman who would like to speak with you out front."

"Can you tell her that I'm with a client, and she will have to come back later?"

"Um, boss I think you really need to take this one. The lady is being very belligerent and disrespectful towards you."

"What do you mean?" Sharnese asked. Renee had her undivided attention now. She didn't know what person in their right mind would come stir up some trouble at her place of business, but she wasn't having it. Whatever drama you had with her on the streets, it stayed there. Once you started messing with her money, it became a problem.

"She's calling you out of your name and everything. I'm trying to keep her from showing off in front of the customers."

"Thank you, Renee," Sharnese said. She made a mental note to give her a raise for staying professional.

"Jessica, can you finish coloring Mrs. Margaret's hair while I go tend to a few things?"

"I got it from here," Jessica replied.

Sharnese wobbled to the front of the salon hoping to get a grasp of what was going on. When she saw the woman rolling her eyes up and down, she was totally confused. "Hi, I'm the owner Sharnese," she said in a professional tone while putting on the fakest smile ever. There was no way she was about to act anything less than classy in her own salon. She had no clue who the woman was, so she couldn't understand the reason for the disrespect. "What can I do for you this morning?" She asked.

Natalie noticed how cool, and unbothered Sharnese was remaining and decided to go another route.

"There's nothing you can do for me, that you're soon to be husband hasn't already done," she said with a big smirk on her face. "There's no need for an introduction I'm sure you know all about who I am. But just in case you don't I'll be more than glad to give you one," Natalie said waiting for a response from Sharnese. "Not only am I your husband's realtor, I'm also the woman who has been screwing your husband's brains out." Sharnese now knew exactly who the woman was. She was finally meeting the woman who she wanted to kill so badly.

"Okay, so that makes you the stalker Natalie, right?" Sharnese said returning the sarcasm. "No, I'm sorry I meant to say the detective. Yes, I know more than enough about you," she said.

Natalie was caught off guard by her last remark. She wasn't expecting her cover to be revealed. She just knew she had covered her tracks so nothing could come back on her, but it was evident that she had been caught up.

"I'm not sure if you recognize it, but you are in my business. You know the place where people make money? Now I have no problem allowing one of my stylists to service you because I don't take money from no one's pocket, but if there's nothing in this salon that we can assist you with, then you need to leave the premises now before things get out of hand," Sharnese said very politely.

Natalie was not about to back down from this confrontation. She had been waiting a long time for the two, to finally meet each other. She saw the way Sharnese rubbed her belly and decided to agitate her a little more. "Isn't it great, how our kids will be around the same age. They'll make wonderful playmates." She said instigating some more. Sharnese's demeanor suddenly changed when she heard that. Her trying to be nice was no longer happening.

"You need to get your purse and get the hell out of here." She glared.

"What's the matter Sharnese? You don't like the fact that Cortez has another baby on the way. I hope it's a boy so I can name him after his father," she taunted.

Sharnese was tired of entertaining her. It was clear that being professional wasn't working, so she had no choice, but to get hood real quick. She went behind the counter and grabbed the revolver from out of the desk drawer. At that time, she wasn't thinking about the clients in the back room as she fired a shot at Natalie's leg missing it on purpose.

"Now, I've told you once before that you need to leave. Don't make me repeat myself because I promise the next time I shoot I won't miss." Natalie's eyes widened in disbelief. She didn't think Sharnese was the type to carry a gun or any weapon for that matter. Natalie had been fooled. Clients came running to the front to see what was going on. Sharnese calmed the women down and reassured them everything was under control. She even gave everyone a discount on getting their hair done to show how sincere she was. As everyone made their way back to their stations, Sharnese stayed where she was. She wasn't going anywhere until Natalie took her ass from out of her salon.

"We'll see each other again. Tell our baby daddy that I miss the feeling of him hitting it from behind. He needs to come feed his child," Natalie said walking out of the salon. She was satisfied with the damage she had done for the day.

Sharnese reached into her apron and dialed Murda's number.

"What's up baby?" He answered on the first ring. Sounding like he was still asleep in the bed.

"Get your ass down to the salon now!" Sharnese screamed into the phone. "Your stalker bitch done came to the salon, got me letting off shots in my place of business. Bring your ass nigga!" Sharnese said hanging up the phone not giving Murda a chance to say anything.

Sharnese went into her office and locked the door until Murda arrived. Renee knocked on the door offering Sharnese something to drink, but she declined. Not even ten seconds later there was another knock at the door. This time it was Murda.

"Sharnese, baby, open up the door, it's me." Sharnese unlocked the door, and Murda stormed in. "Are you okay?" He asked. Tears rolled down her face. Murda went to embrace her, but instead, he was met with a smack across his face. "Yo Nese, I understand you're mad and shit, but I don't put my hands on you, so don't put your hands on me." *Smack!* Another slap landed on the side of his face. "Sharnese chill the fuck out!" He said grabbing a tight grip on her wrists.

"Chill out? You want me to chill the fuck out when you got your bitches coming to my job disrespecting me? Do you know how fucking embarrassed I was having to get all ratchet in front of my clients? You want me to chill out when you out here raw doggin bitches, and getting them pregnant and shit?" Sharnese screamed as more tears threatened to escape her eyes.

"Man, I don't know about none of that shit you over there talking about. When I fucked the bitch I used protection, and that's a fact, so all that baby shit she talking is dead," Murda said trying to plead his case.

Sharnese looked into Murda's eyes, and she could've sworn she saw tears. No matter how much he fucked up, she could never

Bridgette I'esha

find herself staying mad at him for long. She studied the engagement ring on her finger before removing it. "I think we should call off the wedding until we figure this situation out," she said as she placed the ring inside of his hand. It was then that the tears began to roll from Murda's eyes. She had him right where she wanted him. Sharnese knew she was still going to marry his ass, but for the next few minutes, she was about to make him suffer. She wanted him to feel the pain she felt every time she had to be reminded of his infidelity.

"I can't be mad at no one, but myself. After the first incident with Chanel, I should've left yo ass, but no, like a dummy I stayed thinking it was an honest mistake. Boy, did you prove me wrong? Not only did you turn around and fuck another bitch, but you also managed to get another bitch pregnant...or so she says. It was my fault because I played the fool. I allowed it when I should've ended it in the first place. I'm sorry Cortez, but we're officially over."

Murda sat there in the office and cried his heart out. "Sharnese don't leave me. I swear I'm not out here fucking up. I'm just out here trying to get this money so that we can live a good life. That bitch Natalie just jealous because she wants me. I won't answer any of her phone calls. Why else do you think she came here and made a scene? You know the bitch is crazy," he said trying to get his point across.

Sharnese didn't say anything as she gave him the silent treatment for the next few minutes. She continued to remain quiet until Murda got up to walk out the door. "Get yo dumb ass in here and close my door," she said breaking out into a huge grin. "You know I'm not leaving ya ass. I just wanted you to see how I felt. Now put my ring back on my finger," she said as she placed a kiss on his lips.

"I love you Sharnese, and I promise I'm going to do everything in my power to make this situation right."

"I love you too Murda, but you are no longer in charge of handling the Natalie mess. That is now my area. If she thinks she can just march her ass in here, and embarrass me like she did then she got another thing coming." There was no use in protesting against what Sharnese had just said. He knew once she had her mind made up, it was the end of it.

Murda walked Sharnese to the back of the salon, so she could finish Mrs. Margaret's hair. To her surprise, Jessica had gone ahead and styled it for her. Sharnese rescheduled the rest of her appointments for the afternoon as she explained to everyone that she was feeling a little ill. Thankfully no one gave her a hard time, they all understood. She took the rest of the day to go home and to get some much-needed rest.

*****

Natalie drove home from Sharnese's salon happy as hell to have gotten her out of her comfort zone. She knew coming at Sharnese in public would get under her skin, and it did. She was hoping to hear her say that she and Murda were over. The gigantic rock that sat on Sharnese's finger told her everything she needed to know. Sharnese and Murda were still going strong. Natalie couldn't believe that she had been no more than just a simple fuck to him. She'd been calling his phone continuously for months searching for an explanation. All her calls went unanswered and straight to the voicemail. It was bad that it had resulted in her helping the Feds to build a case against him. All he had to do was break her off with a piece of dick here and there, and she would've put him up on all the evidence she had against him. Now she was willing to do anything that may have helped bring him down. She grabbed her phone from out of the cup holder and dialed her boss's number.

"Captain Rivera speaking." He answered on the first ring.

"Hi Captain, this is Detective O'Neal. I have the paperwork on Cortez Rodriguez completed sir," she said into the phone.

"Wonderful, how is everything coming along on your end?" He asked. Natalie had been working undercover for a while, and she was ready to wrap this case up so she could put him away for good.

"Everything's going exactly how we thought it would. He doesn't have a clue that we're on to him," she said nervously. There was no way in hell she was about to tell her boss that her cover had been blown. Not only would the case be thrown out, she would also be demoted. Before she took the assignment, Captain Rivera had stressed to the entire precinct how important it was to take him down. You see Captain Rivera better known as Ricardo to the people in the streets. It was a personal vendetta for him. He had tried to take down Big Jimmy several times back in the day only to fail at every attempt, and be hit with a lawsuit for harassment. He ended up being demoted causing him to lose his home and his wife. Once his wife left with the kids, he had become a drunk until he had got wind of Murda being Big Jimmy's son. After pulling a few strings he was able to get his old position back, and since then he had vowed to take down Murda.

"Great! That's the type of talk I love to hear. Have those papers on my desk first thing Monday morning, so we can work on getting those indictments sent out," he said anxiously. He wanted to move in on him before he slipped through their hands. Captain Rivera knew if Murda was anything like his father, it wouldn't take long for him to sense if something was wrong. For the past two years, the Feds had been trying to build a case against Murda, but they had nothing they could charge him with. Well, that was until he had purchased the real estate through Natalie. With no tax records of ever having a job, they wanted to know where a large amount of money had come from to make the purchase.

"They will be waiting for you first thing in the morning," Natalie assured her boss as she ended the phone call. Natalie's eyes were focused on the road as she continued the drive home. The rain had come from out of nowhere pouring down hard making it extremely difficult to see. It continued to downpour until she was left with no choice, but to pull over and wait for it let up. Her mind wandered back to the conversation she had just minutes before with her boss. She needed more evidence on Murda so that she could keep Captain Rivera off her ass. She immediately dialed Agent Banks's number who she wasn't too fond of. Agent Diamond Banks was one of those people of the law who was crooked as hell. She did anything that she thought would be useful in a case. You better believe if a million dollars was found during a drug raid, only five hundred thousand was being reported. Agent Banks answered the phone in a very seductive tone.

"Hey Natalie babe, how are you?" She said flirting on the other end. She had a big crush on Natalie, and she made sure to display it any time that she could.

"I need you to tap Cortez's phone for me, love," Natalie said playing right along with Diamond's mind games. The line went silent for a few seconds before Agent Banks responded.

"What's in it for me?" She asked. *Nothing in this life is free. She either let me take her out or forget about having access to his phone. It's funny how people only know you when they need or want something from you. She walks passed me every day at work barely even opening her mouth to speak and here she has the nerve to need my help. Humph, we'll just see how this goes.* Agent Banks thought. "I'll help you out…"

"Thank you so much," Natalie said excitedly. She breathed a sense of relief as she knew Agent Banks would make it happen.

"Don't get so happy, you didn't let me finish my sentence before you cut me off."

"I'm sorry go ahead," she said wanting to know what more she could have possibly had to add. Either she was going to do it or not.

"I will help you under one condition."

Here we go with the bullshit. Natalie thought to herself.

"You have to let me take you out on a date." She added.

Natalie rolled her eyes at the top of her head. There was no way in hell she was going on a date with her. She wasn't the least bit interested in her or any other woman for that matter. She was strictly dickly, and Agent Banks needed to just accept that. Natalie weighed her options. Either she goes on the date and gets the information that she needs or she risks losing her job and everything she has worked hard to earn. Since she really needed the evidence, she went ahead and agreed to the dumb arrangement.

Bridgette I'esha

"Alright," she said. "I'll let you take me out."

"Good. I'll have that all set up for you shortly. Have a good weekend."

Natalie ended the call. She started to regret ever asking for her help.

I hope it doesn't take her forever to get this shit done. I'm not trying to be seen out in public with this carpet munching dike. The closest she'll get to taking me out on a date is bringing lunch to the precinct because it isn't happening anywhere else at all.

The rain had stopped, and the once cloudy grey sky had been replaced with a beautiful sunshine. Natalie turned off her windshield wipers and proceeded on her route home. She needed to figure out a way to get Murda's attention. Thirty minutes later she was pulling into the luxurious condo that she called home. She greeted the doorman with a simple smile.

"Good evening Mr. Bill," she said as she checked her mailbox.

"Good evening, Miss Natalie. How are you doing on this brilliant Friday?" He replied.

Natalie didn't mind holding a conversation with Mr. Bill. He had a good spirit about him. No matter what time of day it was, or who else happened to be around, he always made sure to speak to her. He wasn't like the old folks who looked down on the younger generation. Bill was always willing to help her out whether he was signing off on her deliveries or by offering to bring her groceries up the flight of stairs. Bill often said Natalie reminded him of his oldest daughter. She was always working and never had time to enjoy life.

"I'm doing pretty good and yourself?"

"I'm alive and breathing, so I can't complain."

"Mr. Bill, when are you going to retire? I don't want to see you get yourself hurt out here," she said.

Mr. Bill was pushing the age of sixty-five, and he was full of energy. Natalie had never met an older person in such good shape. He could almost move around better than she could.

"I doubt it'll be anytime soon. I don't mind the light work. It gives me something to do. Who wants to be home with a bunch of bad grandkids and kids that think they're your parents? Nope, not I," he said shaking his head.

He had been working in the building for the last ten years. He knew everybody on a first name basis. He probably could tell you their entire schedules too. Mr. Bill was the eyes of the place. He saw everything that went in and everything that came out. You better believe he had no problem reporting any activity that seemed suspicious. Natalie had developed a father-daughter-like a relationship with him over the years. She always appreciated his kind words and wisdom that he would present to her. Often on holidays, Bill found himself eating dinner with Natalie or it was the other way around. Since Bill didn't have a wife, he enjoyed the attention he received from her. He would often tell her that she needed to take a vacation from work and relax more.

"You're a mess, Mr. Bill."

"You had a long day at work, didn't you?" He asked. Mr. Bill was always concerned about her health. He had seen so many young people dying from different types of diseases. He didn't want anything happening to her, especially if it could be prevented.

"Yeah, it's always a long day on the job," she said.

"Well, I'm not going to hold you up. Go on up the stairs, and get you some rest you hear? It's the weekend, go have a drink, and one for me too," he said waving his hand for her to leave.

"Alright Mr. Bill, you take care, and I'll see you later."

Natalie got on the elevator and pressed the button for the twenty-fourth floor. The ride up seemed to take forever. She was ready to unwind and relax a little. After several minutes, the elevator had finally reached her floor. Natalie slowly placed one foot on the carpeted hallway while looking left and right very quickly. Being a detective had taught her to always check her surroundings. It didn't matter that they had surveillance on the premises. Real criminals didn't care what type of crime they committed, or who they committed it against, so she always took precaution. She grabbed her pepper spray from her back pocket as she walked to her door.

Once inside the first thing she did was take off her bra. She didn't want to have it on for a second longer than she had to. She hopped on her Facebook page to see what she had been missing. It wasn't anything, but the usual. She could never understand why people got on social media and told all their business and then got mad once everybody was in it. She scrolled through her timeline seeing nothing, but the same old people with the same old drama. Not feeling the drama, she logged off and debated whether she wanted to call Murda or not. She chose to leave him alone for the time being. She had had enough of the drama with him for one day.

Chapter Nine

I have been following Cortez and his fiancé around for the last few months. It hurt me to my heart to see him and her walking around like a happy couple. It crushed my soul when I saw that she was with child. Here she was living the life I was supposed to have been living. She was in the house that in my mind belonged to me. I don't know how Cortez hadn't realized that someone was on his back. I laughed when I thought about the times I played on his phone, and he called me Natalie. Like who the hell was Natalie? I guess he still had that player mentality after all.

In due time, he would be mines again, and we would start the family that should've been ours from the beginning. It was crazy how a wrong decision could mess up your entire life, and shatter the dreams you so desperately fought hard to hold on to. To make matters worse, everywhere I went they were promoting the wedding they were supposed to have been happening. I had my calendar marked and the day was circled. As long as I was around nobody

was going to be a happy camper. Especially since it wasn't my

wedding. In due time, everything will be mine, and I'm not going

down without a proper fight. Either somebody was going to whoop

my ass or I would be doing the ass whooping during the process. It

had been over twelve years since we last saw each other, and I

didn't know how things would play out once we finally crossed each

other's path. I just hoped that things will work out for the best.

The unknown female watched Murda as he carried a dozen red roses into the house, along with a bouquet of balloons. She wanted to run out of her truck and kiss all over him, but her pride wouldn't allow her to do so. She was just about to drive off when she saw Sharnese open the door. Seeing the happiness that Sharnese displayed was too overwhelming for her. She hated this girl with a passion, and she didn't even know her. All she knew was that Sharnese was with the man that was supposed to have been hers. She waited for them both to disappear from the door. She peeled off down the road. The sight was too much for her to handle.

*****

Bridgette I'esha

Sharnese watered the roses that Murda had given her and smelled them. The red from the roses blended in great with the red & black décor they had in the kitchen. She thought about how distant her and Brooklyn's relationship had become. Brooklyn had always been her favorite cousin up until now. Everyone always warned her about her cousin's deceitful ways, but she tried to look past them. That was until they found out that she had been working with Kas all along. She couldn't believe that the girl she used to share the same bed with as a child had tried to take her life. The betrayal she felt was indescribable, it was like someone had taken a knife and stabbed her dead in the center of her heart. Her mind screamed seek revenge on her, but her heart wouldn't allow her to do so. She decided to leave it in God's hands. She knew one-day Brooklyn would receive whatever was coming her way.

The doorbell rang breaking her from her train of thought. "Babe, can you get the door?" She yelled from the kitchen. Murda was damn near comfortable in the chair. He was not trying to get from out of his spot. "Babe, did you hear me?" She asked peeking from around the corner.

"Yeah Nese, I got it," he replied, placing the blunt inside of the ashtray that sat on the end table. *Damn every time a nigga about to get rest. It's always something that needs to be done. We need a maid around this bitch.*

Murda opened the door to see some foreign looking man standing out front. He sized the man up. Having a man, he was unfamiliar with at his home didn't sit too well with him. "What's good?" Murda greeted the man with a serious mean mug on his face.

"I'm looking for a Sharnese Jackson." The man said rubbing his hands through his long curly hair.

"Who the hell are you?" Murda asked. He didn't appreciate another man coming to his home, and asking for his woman. He stared at the man in front of him real hard. He favored someone very well, but he couldn't think of who.

"I'm Corey…her um…father." He managed to get out. Murda apologized to the man for being so aggressive. He wasn't expecting to hear those words.

"Is she here?" Corey asked.

"Yeah, she's here. I got to warn you. I don't know how she will react to seeing you here," he said giving Corey a heads up.

Bridgette I'esha

"Come inside. No disrespect, but it has been raining today, and I don't want you getting mud all on my white carpet."

Corey accepted Murda's invite inside of the home.

"I don't remember you telling me your name," Corey said.

"It's Mur…Cortez, Cortez Rodriguez," he said extending his hand for a handshake.

Corey shook Murda's hand very roughly. He wasn't too sure about the young man in front of him, but who was he to judge. He had never seen his daughter a day in his life. Often, he wanted to reach out to Mama Peaches, but he figured she would only scowl him like a child, so he left well enough alone. He did, however, visit Tonya in prison once, but she cursed him out so bad he never went back to see her again. It was only recently when Tonya was released did she contact him concerning Sharnese. She had informed him that his only daughter was getting married and that it was time for him to make things right between the both of them. If Sharnese could forgive her mother for the pain and abuse she had put her through, then she could forgive her father for walking out on her and her mother, right?

"Yo, Nese, you have a visitor at the door," Murda hollered out.

"Who is it?" Sharnese asked. She didn't feel like wobbling to the front of the house. The further along she got, the more difficult he became to move around. She was growing tired and becoming irritable. She wasn't in the mood for any company tonight. So, she hoped whoever it was made their visit quick.

"You look even more beautiful than I expected," Corey said staring at Sharnese

She looked over at Murda with confusion. In return, Murda shrugged his shoulders like he didn't have a clue as to what was going on.

"I'll leave you two, to discuss everything," he said as he walked off heading into the direction of the kitchen.

"Who are you?" She asked with her hand placed on her lower back. Her feet were swollen, and her back was killing her.

"I'm your father," he said coming straight out with it.

Sharnese frowned her face. There was no way the man standing in front of her was her father. She had dreamed of meeting him since she was a child. Now she didn't know how she felt. "After almost twenty-four years you finally decide to show your face around here?" She said angrily. She was just about to walk off when Murda appeared from around the corner. He had been eavedropping the entire time.

"Get in there," he said.

"No," she replied poking her lips out and folding her arms like a two-year-old.

"Nese, at least hear the man out. He might have a good explanation as to why he wasn't there when you were a child," he said hoping to have gotten through to her. Sharnese took a minute to think about what Murda had said. She did want to know his reason for leaving her to be raised fatherless.

"Okay," she said agreeing to have a talk with the man who helped create her. *Lord, these people around here are really trying to send me into labor early. It seems like every day my life is becoming even more hectic. Mess around and they are going to commit me to a damn crazy house.*

Sharnese stood there for a few minutes trying to collect her thoughts. After staring at the man who called himself her father, she finally saw why her mother always compared her to him. She was his twin. They shared the same colored eyes and had the same long jet black curly hair. The only difference was her father's Spanish heritage showed more in him.

Corey took a minute to look at his daughter. Her beauty was like no other. Not only did she favor him, she also resembled her grandmother Louise, Corey's mother.

"Sharnese, I want to apologize from the bottom of my heart for not being there for you. To be honest, I wasn't ready to be a father. Back then your mother and I were just kids ourselves. I was too busy running behind different women, trying to be the player of the year. I wasn't the settling down type of man that your mother wanted at the time," he said.

"You could have at least tried to get in contact with me," she said fighting back tears. "I'm not saying things would've been perfect, but at least I would have known that I had a father who cared. You have no clue how hurt I use to be when I would see the girls my age at the father and daughter dances," she said through sniffles.

Corey truly felt bad for neglecting his responsibilities as a father during his younger days. He didn't think about the effect it would have on his daughter. He was too busy being selfish. Running the streets with his boys. Now that he was older he wanted to make up for his absence. He knew it would take some time for her to come around, but that was a risk he was willing to take.

"I'm sorry," he said looking down towards the floor. The guilt he held wouldn't allow him to look her in her face. "If it's okay with you, I would like to make up for all the time we've lost. If you decide not to, then I fully understand," he said hoping she would give him the chance to finally become a part of her life.

Sharnese was unsure of what to say until she saw Murda glaring at her from in the cut. The look on his face told her to give him a chance. "Well, Dad," she said. She felt funny saying those words out loud. She was willing to accept his apology as long as he did right by her this time. "Don't you think we should be getting to know each other a little more?" She said smiling from ear to ear. "I do have a wedding coming up in just a few short weeks. If we can get this right, I would love to have my father walk me down the aisle." She waited for his response. If he took too long to reply then, she would take it as an answer of no. Then she would cut him out of her life forever. Father or no father she was only allowing people in her life, that she felt deserved to be there.

"I would love that," Corey responded.

"Great! You and Cortez can set up a time to go get fitted for your tux. I need you looking like a showstopper if you wish to step foot in my wedding."

Corey looked at all the high-tech and designer things that consumed the house. There was no way he would be able to afford the kind of attire Sharnese expected him to wear. "Listen baby, I see all of the expensive things you have in your house, and from the looks of everything I'm pretty sure you're kicking out a pretty penny for your wedding, but your dad doesn't have that type of money," he said embarrassed that he couldn't afford his daughter's lavish lifestyle.

"Don't worry about it. If you promise to keep up your end of the deal everything is on me. That means no getting ghost on me, and then decide to reappear twenty years later," she said half-jokingly.

"I'm done running away. I can guarantee you that."

"Well, in that case, I'll show you around the house. Have you eaten anything?" She asked.

"I had a slice of pizza earlier today," Corey replied.

"That's not food. Have you ever had the food from Silvia's? It's very tasteful and fulfilling," Sharnese said with her mouthwatering from just thinking about the food. "I'll order us something to eat from there. It's Friday, and I don't do any cooking on the weekends except for Sundays. Plus, as you can see I'm very pregnant, and my appetite varies every day."

Corey replied, "Okay."

"Cortez, will you have Big Ben pick us up a few platters from Silvia's, please love?" She said not giving him a chance to reply.

I'm glad shawty finally got a chance to meet her father and all, but they really fucking up my chill time. Sharnese know every day around this time I like to unwind and smoke my trees. Can't do that with her Pops right there in the other room.

The trio spent the rest of the evening getting to know each other. By the time night had begun, Corey and Sharnese felt like they had been in each other's lives forever. They had just about all the same things in common. There was no denying it. She was her father's child.

"Well, it's about time for me to get going," Corey said taking another shot of Hennessey.

"You leaving already?" Sharnese asked getting used to having her father around. In the couple of hours that he had been there, their bond had grown tremendously. It was a moment she had been waiting on forever.

"Yeah, this old man can't hang with you young folks," he said rubbing her shoulder. "Don't look so sad, this won't be your last time seeing me. It was nice to finally meet you." He turned to his side and looked at Murda. "Son, please take good care of my daughter. Be the type of man that I wasn't able to be for her mother."

Murda shook his head in response. Running out on Sharnese and their unborn child was the last thing he planned on doing.

Sharnese showed her father to the door. Once she saw he was safely in his car, she took a seat on the couch where she ended up dozing off for the remainder of the night.

Bridgette I'esha

Chapter Ten

Brooklyn reached over and hit the snooze button on the alarm clock next to her bed. It was time for her to get up and get ready for her doctor's appointment. She wasn't trying to be caught in the early morning rush hour traffic.

The sunlight beamed through the blinds, putting a strain on her vision. She wiped the hard crust from out of the corner of her eye and yawned. She hated when she had to wake up first thing in the morning. She was not a happy person in the AM. It normally took her a few hours to get herself situated. She was still tired from dancing at the club the night before. She had quickly earned her number one spot back.

Twenty minutes later she was still sitting in the same spot. She headed into the bathroom and took a hot shower. Brooklyn splashed the extra hot water on her face. If nothing else woke her up, then the hot water did as it pierced her skin.

Brooklyn slowly took her time drying off her smooth skin. She lotioned down her body and searched in her closet for her PINK jogging suit. She stared into the floor length mirror which was nailed to her wall. "Ass fat, yeah I know," she said out loud to herself while making each ass cheek bounce one at a time. Everyone swore she had silicone pumped inside of her butt. It was just naturally plump and round. All the women in her family had been blessed with big behinds, so she had them to thank for that asset.

After applying her MAC cosmetics and some clear lip-gloss, she wasn't really into all of the colorful lip products, she pulled her long weave up into a messy bun. She walked outside into her driveway, but couldn't back out due to being blocked in. "Now who the hell is ready to get me off for the day?" Brooklyn asked herself. She blew the car horn hoping whoever was in the car behind her would get the point and move out of her way. When she saw who the driver was that occupied the vehicle, she sucked her teeth loudly. *I am not for his shit today.* She thought to herself as Mark approached her car and tapped on the window. She rolled the window down slightly.

Bridgette I'esha

"What the hell do you want?" She said rudely not in the mood to be dealing with his ass. She was growing sick and tired of him just popping up at her house unannounced and unwanted. No matter how hard she tried to dodge his ass, he was just too persistent.

"Ya fine ass is what I really want," Mark said licking his lips.

Brooklyn gave him the once over. She couldn't deny the fact that he was a fine specimen. His body was cut and ripped. Not an ounce of fat resided there. The tight, form-fitting white t-shirt he had on showed off every muscle on his body. For a minute, she was about to apologize for being so rude, but being nice to everyone was nowhere in her characteristic. She decided to mess with his mind a little bit.

"Let me see what them lips feel like," she said to Mark. As she rolled her window all the way down.

Mark bent down so that he was leveled to her face. He licked his lips again to make sure they weren't dry.

"No need for all of that," Brooklyn said. "Close your eyes for me. I want you to picture these luscious ass lips in your head so you'll never forget them." Mark did as he was told. Once his eyes were closed, Brooklyn hulked up the biggest amount of saliva that she could and spit directly in his face. "I bet ya dumb thirsty ass won't forget that. Now get the fuck out of my way!" She hollered.

"Bitch, I'll kill you for doing' that stupid ass shit!" Mark said as he reached into the car. He wasn't quick enough. Brooklyn had already rolled her window up, and his hand barely missed being caught in the process. Mark kicked Brooklyn's car furiously, leaving a big dent on the back passenger's side. Brooklyn put the car in reserve and backed straight into his A8 Audi. She didn't care about her car being messed up. It could easily be replaced. *One way or another his ass will be moving out of my damn way.* She said to herself, and she continued to back up with even more force.

Mark saw the damage that was being down to his car and decided enough was enough. He hopped in his car and sped out of the driveway. He had to get away from her before he made the first of five news channels. He couldn't understand how such a pretty girl, could have such a nasty ass attitude. All he had been trying to do was make up for the role he played in kidnapping her, but now he was like fuck it. He didn't care what happened to her from here on out. He still hoped that one-day Brooklyn would come to realize that all men weren't out to cause her harm.

Bridgette I'esha

*****

Brooklyn stared at the clock on the wall inside the doctor's office. It was time for her yearly exam. She marched to the receptionist's desk and banged on the glass window.

"Can I help you?" The young black receptionist said with attitude present in her voice.

Brooklyn recognized the girl immediately. It was none other than Skylar. Skylar and Brooklyn had bad blood between the two of them. Skylar blamed Brooklyn for ruining her marriage. She had caught her husband, Jose, spending their rent money on Brooklyn down at the strip club. Skylar called herself trying to act up at Brooklyn's "Job", which ended up being her biggest mistake. Not only did her husband make an ass out of her. He got on the stage and announced to the entire club that he wanted a divorce. To add insult to injury, he left her crying in the middle of the floor while he went to the upper level of the club with Brooklyn. Everybody in the club knew what went down in the rooms up there. Ever since then Skylar hated everything about Brooklyn.

"First you can start by getting rid of your funky ass attitude or I will be speaking with your supervisor. I didn't fuck ya man...at least not last night," Brooklyn said loud enough for the entire office to hear.

Skylar's cheeks flushed red with embarrassment. She didn't need everyone at her workplace knowing her business. Skylar straightened right on up once Brooklyn threatened to report her. Although she wanted more than anything to come from behind the glass and beat Brooklyn's ass, she couldn't risk losing her job. With the way the economy was set up, she knew finding another job with equivalent pay would be near impossible. She bit her tongue and held back the words she really wanted to say.

"Now how much longer do I have to wait before the doctor is ready to see me?" Brooklyn said very loudly trying to cause another scene on purpose.

"As you can see there are plenty of other patients in front of you waiting to be seen," Skylar said pointing to the people in the waiting room.

"I don't give a fuck about none of these bitches in here," Brooklyn said looking everyone that was waiting to be seen in the eyes. She went and took a seat to wait her turn.

"Brooklyn Santana," The nurse called out.

After being in the office for two hours, she was finally ready to be seen. Brooklyn had given Skylar an evil glare before she was hit with another surprise. It was none other than Vonsha. *If I see another bitch I can't stand around this muthafucka I'm going the fuck off.* Brooklyn thought to herself.

Vonsha stood at 5'6 with honey blonde locks. She was a little on the thick side, but she was far from what you would consider being fat. A devious smile appeared on her face as she looked over Brooklyn's charts. Like every other female, Vonsha and Brooklyn couldn't get along. In the little time that Brooklyn had spent in high school, she and Vonsha were rivals. They were always competing against each other in something. Boys, who could dress the best, who had the latest hairstyle and other typical stuff that females fought over.

"Stand on the scale so that I can check your weight and height," Vonsha demanded rather than asking.

Brooklyn looked at her like she had lost her mind. "I know damn well ya ass ain't talking to me like that," she said turning around to see if somebody else was in the room with them. "You know I have no problem beating ya ass on ya job," Brooklyn said hoping she was bold enough to try it.

Vonsha rolled her eyes. This was the main reason she wanted a job far away from where she was from. She hated running into people she knew didn't like her. It was a local clinic, and everybody and their momma came there for checkups. One thing about Vonsha was she knew how to remain cool under pressure. She wasn't about to feed into Brooklyn's dumb shit. She already knew how Brooklyn got down.

"Brooklyn, don't nobody have time to be playing games with you. Just get on the scale so that I can do my job," Vonsha said with pleading eyes.

Brooklyn knew she had to be crazy for real to think she gave a damn about her job. There was no way in hell Vonsha was getting away with talking to her out the side of her neck.

"Don't think I won't haul off and smack the hell out of ya ass on ya job. One thing's for sure two things for certain I don't give a fuck about you! Now hurry up, and finish before I decide to yell real loud and make it seem like you're doing something to me and you know I WILL do it." Vonsha hurried up and finished the task at hand.

Being the spiteful person, she was, Brooklyn hollered at the top of her lungs like someone was trying to kill her. "Help! Help! Somebody, please come quickly, she's hurting me," screamed Brooklyn.

The doctor rushed into the room almost tripping over the stool. "What is going on in here?" Dr. Peterson asked sternly while staring at Vonsha.

"Your nurse just pushed me off this scale. I think I might have twisted my ankle," Brooklyn said playing like she was hurt.

"Is this true Vonsha?" Dr. Peterson asked. He was very strict about professionalism in his office. He would fire you in a heartbeat, and then wait for you to file your claim for unemployment just to deny your benefits.

"Now you know I never act anything, but professional while I'm on the job," she said as her voice began to crack.

"She's lying. If something isn't done about this right fucking now, I will be suing the hell of this company."

Brooklyn now had his undivided attention. The last thing he wanted to do was give up money over a problem that could have easily been avoided. "Vonsha, can you go and get Miss Santana's health records? Then, once you're done, you can take the rest of the day off to think about the actions you've displayed in my office." Vonsha smiled, but on the inside, she was mad as hell.

"I'll get right on it," she replied still mad that she would be losing days' worth of pay behind Brooklyn's dumb ass.

While Vonsha was in the next room printing Brooklyn's file from off the computer, she stumbled across Brooklyn's results for her HIV test. She thought her eyes were deceiving her until she reread the results again. In big bold letters were the words HIV positive. Vonsha didn't have a bit of sympathy in her body for Brooklyn's scandalous ass as she thought about all the evil things Brooklyn had done to her out of spitefulness. After reading Brooklyn's results, she was more than happy to hand them over to Dr. Peterson. As much as she wanted to wait around to see the look on Brooklyn's face, she knew Dr. Peterson would never allow it. He took pride in making sure his patients had confidentiality.

"Here you go," Vonsha said as she handed him the files. She felt like Brooklyn deserved everything that was bound to come her way. Brooklyn walked around like her shit didn't stink, but how funny was it now that the tables were about to turn.

"Thank you, I'll see you in the morning. Hopefully, by then your attitude and job performance will be up to par with everything else inside of this facility."

Vonsha didn't say a word as she left out of the room. She wasn't the only one who was about to have a bad day. Brooklyn was about to receive the worst news of her entire life.

Dr. Peterson read over Brooklyn's chart and remained quiet for a few seconds. This was the part his job he disliked the most. "Brooklyn, how many sex partners have you had within the last year?" He asked in a serious tone.

She shrugged her shoulders in a nonchalant way. "I don't know. I mean who actually keeps a track of that." Brooklyn had messed around with so many different men, she probably could only remember the name of one. Most of the time, she never even bothered asking them for their names. The only names she wanted to hear come from out of a man's mouth were Franklin, Grant, and Jackson.

"Miss Santana, this is very serious not only for your health but for the health of the many others you may have infected. I'm sorry to say this, but according to your test results you tested positive for the HIV virus."

Brooklyn felt like the walls were closing in on her. Her breathing became shallow as she tried to speak, but no words came out. "There must be a mistake," she said to the doctor.

"Our records indicate that the last time you were here your test results came back positive. Now, I can send them off to be viewed again," Dr. Peterson said. He really did feel sorry for her.

At that time, Brooklyn was mad at the world. She waited until he finished explaining the next process. After everything had been said and done, Brooklyn was advised to come back every six months to be tested again. Brooklyn walked out of the doctor's office, her heart colder than what it already was. It was no telling who she had contracted the disease from, and for that reason alone she would make every man in the world pay. The only thing on her mind was to spread the disease to as many men and she possibly could. She went home to get some rest before work that evening. Work that night would be the biggest money-making night in history. Since she had the disease, everyone in the state of New York would have it too. Nobody was off limits. If bitches wanted to remain HIV free, then they should've started with making sure their men were faithful.

That night at the club, history was made. The club's owner Ricky had never seen so much money made in the VIP rooms. He didn't know what had inspired Brooklyn to go so hard, but he loved it. Men were literally lined up outside of the room waiting for their turn with her. Brooklyn walked from out of one of the back rooms and ran straight dead into Ricky.

"Paradise, how are things going tonight?" He asked.

"Same shit, different day. Just busting this pussy open for a few bucks. That's all."

Ricky laughed at Brooklyn's remark. He loved how she was always so blunt. She always said anything that came to her mind. No caring where she was at, or who she was talking to.

Bridgette I'esha

"I just wanted to let ya ass know that I salute ya hustle. I see you out here grinding' tonight, working hard for dem dollars."

"Thanks…I guess?" Brooklyn said unsure of how to take Ricky's compliment.

Ricky was only congratulating Brooklyn in hopes that she would break him off with some ass before the night was over with. "I ain't trying to fuck up ya money or whatever, so I'll let you get back to doing you."

Brooklyn smiled as she walked away leaving Ricky standing in the hallway.

If only he knew where my inspiration came from. I'm sure his ass would not have been congratulating me. She thought to herself as she went to go freshen up. She had plenty more customers to infect before the night was over.

Chapter Eleven

Murda sat at the head of the table. He briefly took the time to examine each of the men he'd put in high ranks. He and Money both had some important news to share with the family. They didn't know how well it would play out, but they were ready for whatever came their way.

Murda made sure he chose his words very carefully before he spoke. "Family, the day has come for Money and I to resign for a bit." The room was still silent, so he continued. "Yes, for the last eight years we've provided Brooklyn with some of the purest cocaine the fiends have ever seen. We've invested our money in numerous amounts of businesses. As you all may be aware, I have an ongoing beef in the streets with that nigga Kas. After several attempts of trying to take him out, I've still been unsuccessful. So, with that being said, I will be taking the timeout to handle that situation, and hopefully for good. Money and I have been doing this for quite some time now, and we both realize that we can't be in these streets forever. So, with, Money and I will now be turning everything over to Pop."

Pop's eyes widened in astonishment. This was not something he was expecting. Murda and Money saw how much he applied himself when putting in work. Over the law few months, they had watched him morph into a man from being a little boy, so they knew they were making the right decision. Everyone in attendance remained quiet. It was against the rules to allow them to keep breathing, but nobody wanted to go against the two men who had always been good to them. The same ones who made sure nobody ever went hungry. Money and Murda had always shown love, so the team felt obligated to show love back. Everyone nodded their heads in the direction of their ex-bosses, agreeing to the new arrangements.

"Pop, come and take your seat on the throne," Money yelled out to Pop.

"Always stay the same. Don't let the money change you, or the fame betray you. Be sure to assess the situation first before responding. There will always be someone in the crowd watching, preying on your downfall," Money said to Pop hoping that he

Bridgette I'esha

listened wisely to the words he had just said. Money was a man of few words, so when he spoke it was important to take heed.

Pop didn't understand why he had just whispered a speech in his ear until he saw everyone congratulating and showing love except his main man Rich. *This nigga can't possibly be throwing shade right now, especially when I've always looked out for him.* Pop thought to himself. He knew niggas with bitch traits came along with the money, power, and respect, but he would've never expected it to come from his A1 dawg, Rich. He and Rich were as tight as brothers. They went as far back as the sandboxes, eating Ramen Noodles and running around with snotty noses. Pop couldn't understand why he was acting the way he was. Pop walked over to Rich, so he could feel him out.

"You good, blood?" Pop asked him.

Rich stood with his back against the wall. He didn't even bother to look at Pop while he was speaking to him. That alone was blatantly disrespectful. Rich's whole disposition was nasty as hell, but Pop chose to ignore it. It was his day of celebrating, and he wasn't about to let Rich or anybody else take that from him.

"Check it, I'm about to bounce on out of here. I'll get up with you sometime tomorrow," Rich said as he left the celebration. Not once did he congratulate Pop on his new position.

Pop went back to mingle with some of his family in attendance. After seeing with his own eyes, the hate, he was receiving from his right-hand, he needed some trees to smoke. Pop could smell the scent of weed from a mile away as it lingered above his nose.

"Yo, who got that loud around this muthafucka?" He said as he went searching for the culprit.

*****

Murda and Money were in the corner observing everything that was taking place. They knew this was a major accomplishment for Pop, but they still needed him to be focused at all times. You never knew when shit would jump off. In this game, you had to have eyes in the back of your head. At any given second shit could get real. It didn't matter who you were around. You could never get too comfortable. It was a dog eat dog world, and no matter how much family or friends claimed to have your back at the end of the day everyone was out for themselves.

Bridgette I'esha

They saw how the entire conversation went down. Money wanted to go over and check Rich for being in his feelings, but Murda quickly stopped him.

"He a grown ass man, let him handle that shit," Murda said with his eyes still glued on the pair. He knew Pop was more than capable of holding his own. He knew if it came down to him and Rich taking it to the streets, Pop's trigger game was official.

Money knew Murda was right. It wouldn't look good on Pop's behalf if Money jumped into some shit that had nothing to do with him.

"You right, let me get the fuck back before I fuck around and make a bad situation worse."

Money wasn't too fond of Rich. From the very first moment, he met him he felt something wasn't right, and he always went with his first instinct which hadn't let him down yet. Nonetheless, Rich was Pop's man, and it was a problem he would have to deal with alone unless it got out of hand.

"Do that, because I got enough shit going on over my way. A nigga can't afford any more run-ins with the law," Murda said as he ran his hand over his long goatee that he decided to let grow. Murda had been stressing like crazy. He still hadn't figured out what Natalie had going on. He was growing tired of wondering when they were finally going to make their presence known, letting them know that a case was being built. He just hoped he would get to witness the birth of his son first.

"What the fuck is going on, bruh?" Money asked. "Have you heard from shawty lately?"

"Nah, that's the crazy part. The bitch has been quiet as hell lately, and that's the shit that scares me. I don't know whether to be jumping for joy or be trying to dig up some shit. You know the saying; no news is good news?"

"Yeah," Money said nodding his head, unsure of where Money was headed with the conversation.

"Well then, I'ma leave it the hell alone," Murda chuckled even though the situation with Natalie was far from a laughing matter. On several occasions, he thought about calling her so that he could dick her down, but he thought better of it. He was already skating on thin ice with Sharnese, and he knew his get out of jail free cards were winding down.

Money knew his friend all too well. It was only a matter of time before some kind of female drama came his way.

"Man, it doesn't even seem like we just handed over our throne," Money said. He planned on spending as much time as he could with Destiny and their baby girl London.

"Shit man, I was saying the same thing to myself," Murda replied. With the spare time he had on his hands, he was ready to expand his real estate some more. He wanted property everywhere. It was time for him to make more moves out of state. He wanted to own property in several different locations, so if he ever felt like he was in one spot for too long, he could jump up, and leave whenever he wanted.

"For real, I just stopped moving weight, but I'm still deep in these streets, and I will continue to be as long as dat nigga Kas is walking the around. He should've been six feet under a long time ago. I don't know what the fuck is going on with me, bruh."

Murda felt like a failure. In the past year, he had two attempts on his life by the same person, and the nigga that made them was still breathing.

"How is shit coming along with getting ya son back?" Murda asked changing the entire conversation. He was glad he didn't have to deal with the baby mama drama. He saw how hard Money grinded to provide for his son. To see him have to go through the bullshit, he understood why some men just paid child support and left it at that. No matter how much you did for your child, it would never be enough to a woman that still wanted you.

"Man, I still can't believe the bitch had me arrested for assault and battery. If I would've known, I was gonna go to jail, I would've really considered whipping her ass."

Murda choked off the Paul Mason he was drinking. He couldn't see his boy going in on his baby mom, but he knew if provoked, Money would have no problem with putting his paws on her.

Money still wasn't done venting. He needed a man to see his point of view. Talking to Destiny wasn't something he could do all the time. Especially since she hated Brooklyn just as much as he did.

"Her doing shit like that is the exact reason I got to get my son out of that environment. Here he has been gone for these months, and she's made no effort to bring him home. If she knows all she wants to do is slut around, then she might as well sign her damn rights over." Brooklyn reminded Money of his own mother which was probably one of the reasons why he had so much resentment towards her. He didn't want his son growing up thinking it was okay for women to act the way Brooklyn did. He wanted his son to respect women, and Brooklyn was not showing him that.

"You good, yo?" Money asked.

"I'm straight dawg, good looking though," he said still trying to recover from choking. "You just got one nut ass baby mama son," Murda said.

Money was about to respond when his cell phone started vibrating. It was only Destiny wanting to know when he was bringing his ass home. She had this rule that once she locked the doors for the night, nobody got in unless they had a key.

"Looks like I'm a have to wrap this conversation up. You know how it goes when wifey calls, and a nigga sure ain't trying to have Destiny's crazy ass pissed off. Fuck around and she try to shoot me with my own gun," Money said half-jokingly. He knew Destiny would try it.

"I'm about ready to dip out myself," Murda replied. "I hate Nese being at the house alone."

"What happened to Ben? He ain't security no more?" Money asked.

"Nothing happened. He's still on the job. I just feel at ease when I'm there with her. Shit, she could go into labor at any minute, and I'll be damn if I want another nigga looking at my pussy."

Money fully understood where Murda was coming from. He would get uptight whenever the doctor had to check Destiny's private areas, so he couldn't do anything but agree with him.

After Money and Murda were finished wrapping up their conversation, they both hopped into their vehicles and headed in the directions of their homes where the women they loved awaited them.

Chapter Twelve

Cause what you gonna do

When I put that pretty thing on you

I usually don't do this, but I'll do it for you

Oh baby, cause missing you is way too hard to do

I'd rather be fucking you

Do you mind if I give you love?

Cause I just want to give you love

Won't you tell me if I'm doing too much?

Missing you is way too hard to do...

Destiny sang along with K. Michelle as she happily danced around her bedroom. She had won her first case in court earlier that day. All the charges against Money were dropped, and he was found innocent after she submitted the videotape. Once the jurors reviewed

Bridgette I'esha

the evidence presented to them, they were appalled. Brooklyn had portrayed herself to be the liar that she was. The tape clearly showed that Money was indeed home when the assault on Brooklyn took place. In the end, Brooklyn was found guilty of providing the police with false information, and charged with perjury. Although they had won this battle, Money still had another court date coming forth for the custody of their son, Sincere.

Destiny took a sip from the Amaretto Ciroc that she was drinking on. For her, it was a celebration. Ever since she was a little girl, she dreamed of one day owning her law firm and becoming a successful lawyer. Although this was only her first case, she felt unstoppable. This was just what she needed for her business to grow. By the time next year rolled around she had planned to have another firm open down in the south, Georgia to be exact. With hard work and dedication, she was destined for greatness.

Money crept up behind her not saying a word. He stood back and admired every curve on Destiny's body. In his eyes, Destiny was a blessing. You couldn't find too many other women that went hard for what they wanted out of life. He literally watched her start from the bottom and make her way up to the top.

Bridgette I'esha

When he first met Destiny, she was ratchet as hell! Loud, bright colored weave, the whole nine yards. At first, he could never see himself with her exclusively, but once he got to know her, he saw that the person she portrayed on the outside was nothing like the person she really was. She was still hood, but she had goals she wanted to achieve in life. When she first told him, she was in school on a full scholarship to become a lawyer he laughed. He never expected her to say that, so he didn't take her seriously until she started declining his invites to catch a movie, or just to hang out. It was then he became her study partner, quizzing her on any assignment she would have a test on. Now here he was a living witness to what could happen if you put your mind to it. Not only was he her husband, but also her first client.

"You feeling yaself, huh?" Money asked. Destiny turned around damn near twisting her ankle in the process.

"The liquor got me feeling good that's all," she replied. The effects of the alcohol had her thinking she was one of Chris Brown's backup dancers. Money couldn't help but laugh at Destiny as she continued to vibe to the music in the mirror. She walked over to Money and dropped it low while singing along with the chorus, "Do

you mind if I give you love? Cause I just want to give you love?"
She sang her heart out to him. Destiny truly loved Money. He had
been there for her when no one else was there. They had built an
empire that she felt no woman could break. Money always made her
feel like she was the only woman attractive enough for his eyes. The
best part about their relationship was that they motivated each other
to go further in life. Money pushed Destiny to the highest mountain
to pursue her dreams while Destiny encouraged him to start his own
business and to leave the street life alone.

Money picked Destiny up and carried her over to the bed. He
removed every inch of clothing that was on his body and hers. He
was ready put in work. Destiny was a straight freak once the alcohol
got into her system. She climbed on top of him and placed a trail of
kisses from lips and stopped just above his waist. She looked into
Money's eyes and licked her lips. He already knew what time it was
and couldn't wait. Destiny had a mean ass head game. Once she
placed her lips on his shaft, it was a wrap. Up and down she bobbed
her head pleasuring her man. Money grabbed the back of Destiny's
head and wished he hadn't.

"Why the hell did you stop?" He asked breathing hard and out of breath.

"Nigga, I don't need you guiding me. I'm a pro, I got this," she said rolling her eyes. Destiny hated when Money did that. It made her feel like she didn't know what she was doing.

"My bad Des, damn. Shit, you got a nigga over here feeling good and shit. Ya head shouldn't be so damn good. I couldn't control myself."

Rolling her eyes, she said, "Can I get back to what I was doing without any help? When I need your help, I'll ask."

"Yeah, whatever," Money said agreeing with Destiny. He just wanted her to put her mouth back to work. His man was throbbing uncontrollably.

Destiny went back to bobbing her head. Money moaned loud as the slurps coming from Destiny's mouth grew louder and louder.

"Ahh, slow down Destiny," he said.

Destiny could feel him extending. There was no way she was about to let him finish and not get hers. She continued for a few more seconds before getting up and lying flat on her back. Money positioned himself over top body and entered her secret garden.

Destiny's pussy was just the way he liked it, shaved, tight and clean with no odor. The size of Money's dick filled her walls to capacity. She clenched her teeth when he first entered inside of her. She wrapped her legs around his waist, wanting all of him. Money kissed Destiny's neck which drove her crazy. She let out moans that caused him to pump furiously. Five minutes later Money was releasing all his kids inside of her. They both got up and took a shower together. Afterward, they drifted off to paradise in each other's arms.

Chapter Thirteen

Murda stood outside of the church socializing with a few men that were in the wedding which was scheduled to take place within the next hour. He couldn't wait to marry the love of his life. Sharnese had been his lover, friend, and his soldier. You couldn't find too many women that were willing to put up with a man fucking up all the time, but she did. She didn't need a man in her life, but she deserved a good one. Life had dealt her some fucked up cards, but in the end, she came out on top. Murda was impressed with the progress they had made in their relationship. It hadn't been an easy ride. Sharnese had stood by him through everything. She was there during his near-death experience, and she dealt with all the drama that had come from his side chicks. Murda loved everything about Sharnese. Her smile would brighten the darkest room. She was his down ass chick. There wasn't a woman in the world he had ever shown so much love and affection to besides his mother.

Sharnese was his backbone, and he loved the hell out of her. She was the only woman who could talk shit, whip his ass, and get away with it. He felt like he was making the best decision of his life. Besides he needed someone who understood his lifestyle, and everything that came with it. Even though he had given it up. Murda wanted to be with her forever. He knew if anything was to happen to him, then she would have no problem with holding everything down and taking care of business.

Money emerged from the church and went to stand beside Murda. The tailored made suit he wore made him look just like the boss he was. Money wanted to feel Murda's vibe out before he took that big step. "How's everybody doing this afternoon?" He said not speaking in his usual street slang. Everyone greeted him back with the same response.

"We good over here." They all said in unison.

"How you feeling, bruh?" Money asked while playfully slapping Murda on the back.

Although he would never admit it, nervousness was written over his entire face, but he played it cool and replied, "Everything is everything." Murda was not about to let anyone see him sweat. His stomach was doing all kinds of knots and flips as the time winded down.

The guests were being ushered into the white chapel to take their seats. The seating process was taking a little longer than expected due to everyone having to sign in and show their invitations. Brooklyn and Kas were amongst the small crowd waiting to be escorted to their seats. The new do Kas had must have been working since he managed to get through undetected by the security that was at the door. Kas removed the rubber band from his long dreads and let them hang down his back. The Prada glasses he wore helped conceal his identity, hiding his light brown eyes.

"Brooklyn don't fuck this up for us," Kas reminded her. Forgetting they were inside of the Lord's house.

Brooklyn cut her eyes over at him. She only wanted to hear him say that he had her money waiting for her. She didn't care what happened after those dead presidents sat pretty in her hands. Since finding out she was HIV positive, her heart had become even colder than what it was before. She had a fuck the world and everybody in it mentality.

"As long as you have that dough like you say then you don't have to worry about me fucking up. Now let you not have it…well, you'll see what happens when you create beef with Brooklyn," she said not attempting to hide the fact that she'd just threatened him.

Kas continued to mumble a few words under his breath hoping he wouldn't draw any attention to them. Brooklyn tuned him out while she scanned the church looking for her next potential victims.

*****

Sharnese looked absolutely stunning in her Vera Wang maternity wedding gown. The makeup on her face was flawless. This was the happiest moment of her life. She hadn't seen her soon to be husband in two days, and it was killing her. All she kept doing was wondering who he was with, what he was doing, and if he was out cheating. She pushed those crazy thoughts to the back of her head. Wiping a piece of hair from out of her face she drank some of the ice-cold water that rested on the table in front of her.

Her stomach growled viciously as she hadn't had anything to eat since the night before. The way her pregnancy was set up nausea would hit her at any time, and she wasn't trying to have any mishaps with her dress. The photographer was in the center of the floor positioning the bridesmaids so that he could get their pictures taken for the album.

Every one of them looked gorgeous, but of course not better than the bride. All the girls had the exact same style dresses on along with the same shoes. Sharnese had made it clear to all of them. If anyone of them had worn anything besides what had been ordered, then they wouldn't be allowed to partake in the wedding ceremony. It was her wedding so her rules. Simple as that.

"I need everyone in their places," said Cia, the wedding coordinator. "All of the guests are seated, and we shall be starting momentarily." Cia had done a wonderful job with decorating the church. She was one of the best party planners in the state of New York. It didn't matter what type of event it was, she delivered nothing but complete satisfaction.

"Sharnese, Hun, are you ready?" Cia asked while doing a once over of everyone. The strapless dresses the bridesmaids were wearing complimented each one of the different shapes and sizes of the women.

Sharnese was trying hard to shake the nervousness that she felt. Her hands were shaking rapidly as her heart fluttered a few times. She took another sip of water hoping that it would help relax her a bit.

"Yeah, I'm ready. I just wish I could get rid of this nervous feeling I have," she replied.

Cia knew exactly how to fix the anxiety Sharnese was feeling. She suffered from the same problem from time to time.

"Take a deep breath. Think about all the good memories you and your soon to be husband shared together."

Sharnese closed her eyes and did as she was told. Immediately her body released the tension which had tightened her body in the first place.

"Did it help any?" Cia asked, more than ready to get the wedding started. She couldn't wait for them to see how everything had been put together.

"It did. Thanks, Cia, you're the best," said Sharnese.

Cia blushed at the compliment. She gathered the girls up and placed them in order for the lineup. Sharnese was still waiting in the office when she heard a slight knock at the door.

Bridgette I'esha

"It's open," she replied wishing that it was Murda. Instead, it was her father, Corey. Sharnese couldn't believe her eyes. Corey cleaned up very well. She and Murda had purchased him an all-white Armani suit, and he looked good in it.

"Hey dad," Sharnese greeted Corey. It had taken her some time to get used to saying those words. It damn sure didn't happen overnight. Corey was amazed at how beautiful his daughter was. She looked like a princess from out of a fairytale story.

"Hey baby girl," Corey replied with watery eyes. "Thank you for allowing me the privilege to share this special moment with you," he said while grabbing a hold of Sharnese's hands.

"No need to thank me. Trust me when I say it's a pleasure having you here with us," Sharnese said dabbing away at the tears rolling down the side of her face. "Now dad, I love you in all, but you got to leave. You got me in here messing up my makeup," she said trying to apply her cosmetics to the area that was smudged a little.

Corey just stood there staring at Sharnese. He couldn't believe he had missed out on her entire life. He often found himself wondering how things would've been if he'd stayed all those years ago. Corey and Sharnese's conversation was cut short when Cia walked in.

"Corey and Sharnese, we're ready for you," Cia said.

Sharnese grabbed a hold of her father's hand very tightly as they walked out of the door. It was a dream come true. She had always imagined that one day her father would be next to her walking her down the aisle, and now she was living it out. The church was filled to its capacity.

"Everyone, please stand as we wait for the entrance of the bride," Cia said as she opened the doors to the sanctuary. Sharnese walked in with the sounds of Case singing *Happily Ever After* in the background. All eyes were rested on her. There at the altar stood the man of her dreams. She could feel him staring her down from where he was. She took her time walking, and she thought about how her life would change forever. Mama Peaches was seated in the front pew. She smiled at her granddaughter as she made her way down the aisle. Sharnese had done what no woman in their family had ever managed to do, settle down.

Finally, at the altar, Sharnese stood face to face with her confidant. The preacher greeted everyone in attendance.

"Thank you, family and friends, of both the bride and the groom for being here with us this afternoon as we celebrate the becoming of one and the love these two people have in their hearts for one another. Sharnese and Cortez, you are promising the people you love that you want to be with only each other for the remainder of your lives. Let me tell you this, marriage will not be a walk in the park. You will face difficult times, and this will be no easy task. But with God as your savior, you two will have the power to overcome all obstacles you may face. Who will do the honor of giving this young lady away?" Asked the Preacher.

"I will," Corey said as he stepped in front of the pulpit.

The preacher then turned to face Murda and said the following, "Cortez, will you take Sharnese to be your lawfully wedded wife, to stand by her side through sickness, and health till death do you part?"

"I do," Murda replied. He didn't need to think about the question being asked. He would've never asked Sharnese for her hand in marriage if he didn't want to be with her forever. Murda had made some mistakes in their relationship that he was ready to make right. He swallowed hard as he tried his best to fight the tears that

Bridgette I'esha

were trying to fall from his eyes. The woman he was ready to commit himself to had captured his heart from the first day he had laid eyes on her. It was something about her that intrigued him, and he couldn't explain it. Murda smiled at Sharnese, and in return, she did the same.

The preacher went on to repeat those same exact words he had just spoken to Murda to her. "Sharnese will you take Cortez, to be your lawfully wedded husband to stand by his side through sickness and health till death do you part."

"I do," Sharnese replied. She stood at the altar crying like a big baby as her emotions got the best of her. She and Murda didn't even wait for the preacher to continue the sermon before they pressed their lips against one another and kissed. The guests stood and clapped as they watched the beautiful union taking place.

Murda placed Sharnese's ring on her finger. The diamonds glistened as the reflection shined from the chandeliers hanging above their heads. It was now Sharnese's turn to do the same. Murda was impressed with the ring. It was his first time seeing it, and he had to give his wife her props. She had exquisite taste. It was definitely something he would've picked out on his own.

"Is there anyone who feels that these two should not wed in holy matrimony? Speak now or forever hold your peace."

It was either now or never, Journee said to herself. "Wait, Cortez! You can't marry her. We have a thirteen-year-old daughter together," she shouted.

Murda looked to see where the commotion was coming from. His eyes rested upon a familiar face. "Journee?" He questioned. He wasn't sure if it was her or not. He hadn't seen Journee since their high school years and here she was now sabotaging his wedding. He didn't know whether to be happy about his childhood sweetheart or mad as hell.

"Yes baby, it's me and this is your daughter Armani," she said pointing to the young girl who stood beside her. There was no denying that the girl looked like Murda. They shared the same green eyes and long black hair.

"Journee, you need to leave now! Out of all days, you wait until today to pull a stunt like this? Security please remove her from the premises."

"But what about our daughter?" She asked.

"We will not discuss this here. Now I'm asking you nicely. Don't make me get nasty," Murda said getting himself worked up.

Big Ben and another man escorted Journee and her daughter out the front doors, but not before Journee had a chance to shout, "This is not over!"

Sharnese felt sick to her stomach. She couldn't believe the drama that was unraveling on her wedding day. Once again there was drama involving Murda and another woman. Only this time she couldn't fault him. The woman had waited thirteen years to show her face and mention a daughter she claimed to be her husbands. She really had a lot of nerve.

Destiny did what any friend would've done in a situation like this. She ran over to Sharnese's side. She didn't say a word as she comforted her best friend. No words were needed as she had witnessed everything with her own two eyes.

Murda didn't know what to do about the current situation at hand. He loved Sharnese, but he felt old flames beginning to resurface. He shook those feelings off as he went to console his wife.

"I'm sorry Sharnese," he said holding her in his arms. "I really didn't know. Let's just continue on with our wedding."

Bridgette I'esha

Sharnese didn't say a word. She had just been humiliated in front of her family and friends. She knew this would be the most talked about topic for the next few days. She was starting to have second thoughts about getting married. Maybe it just wasn't meant for them to be together, but she really loved him and all the drama that came with him. Sharnese stared at Murda. Her eyes were cold as ice while she said the following words. "From this day forward, if I hear about you entertaining another female it's over for good," she said while getting herself together.

"May I continue?" Asked the preacher who was becoming very irritated? He had another wedding he needed to be at shortly, and they were prolonging him with the drama.

Murda and Sharnese looked at each other, and in agreement, they both said, "Yes."

"I now pronounce you husband and wife. You may now kiss the bride."

Kas looked over at Jermaine and on cue, the two stood up and opened fire. Screams echoed throughout the sanctuary. Guests were running around trying to find an exit. Sharnese dropped hard to the floor. She didn't know what to do as the church was in complete chaos. She looked up and saw Mama Peaches, her mother, and father. She felt a sense of relief when she saw they were okay.

Boom! Boom! Boom! Boom! The sounds of Kas's .45 Magnum could be heard throughout the entire church. Murda ducked down, but not before being able to see that Kas was the intruder that was causing a bunch of mayhem. This was the one-day Murda didn't have his gun on him, and he was pissed. He never went anywhere without it, but being that he was in a church he didn't feel the need to carry it on him. He crawled across the floor scrambling to make his way to Sharnese.

Chapter Fourteen

As the two crews exchanged gunfire, many innocent people lost their lives in the bloody massacre. Dead bodies were sprawled throughout the entire sanctuary. What was supposed to have been a day of celebration had turned into an evening of mourning. Murda completely neglected his own safety as he barely dodged the bullets flying across his head trying to protect the love of his life from raining bullets. Sharnese was laid face down on the church's floor.

"Nese are you hit?" He asked as he searched her body for any wounds. None was there. He continued to search her bloodstained wedding dress, but couldn't figure out where the blood had come from. Once again, he called out to Sharnese. "Nese, were you hit?"

"No," she said in a faint tone. "I think something is wrong with the baby. I'm bleeding Murda," she replied with tears running down her face. Her body shook uncontrollably as she sobbed. Murda said a prayer to the man above asking him to watch over his unborn son and wife. His only concern now was getting her out of there alive.

Boom! Boom! Boom! More gunfire continued to erupt throughout the sanctuary. When Murda looked up, he was shocked to see Natalie aiming her gun in the direction of Sharnese. With these witnesses around Murda knew there was no way possible he could get away with killing a detective in broad daylight. He was asking for the police to be on his ass if he did. Natalie took turns pointing her gun back and forth between Murda and Sharnese. Sharnese stared directly into her eyes unafraid of death.

Murda searched around for Kas's gun, but it was too late. Natalie had already pulled the trigger. Murda felt his stomach twisting in knots. He was sure Sharnese was dead. He refused to look in her direction as he feared the worst. When he finally did look his heart sunk to the bottom of his stomach. Brooklyn was one of the victims caught in the crossfire. A bullet hole rested between the middle of her eyes while blood poured from her mouth. It was the last thing Sharnese needed to see. She was already on the verge of an emotional breakdown. Natalie had tried to shoot Sharnese, but instead, she missed and shot Brooklyn instead.

Bridgette I'esha

Sharnese was very weak, but she managed to pick up the gun beside her. With her hands trembling, she lifted the gun. Natalie was so busy worrying about Murda she never saw her life flash before her eyes. Her body jerked as it hit the ground. Sharnese had fired a shot that left a permanent hole in Natalie's chest.

Money came from out of nowhere firing shots from his Ak-47. BLAT! BLAT! BLAT! BLAT! The artillery was so powerful it ate Kas's body alive. Several parts of his body were dismembered and scattered around the church.

"Give me those guns, and get the hell out of her now! There's a truck waiting for you two outside. Destiny is already in there." Money noticed the large stain of blood on Sharnese's dress. "Get her to a hospital quick."

Murda scooped Sharnese up in his arms as he made their escape out the doors. Sure, enough Big Ben was in the driver's seat and Destiny was signaling for him to pull off.

Sharnese was in extreme pain. She struggled to speak but managed to get out what she had to say. "Murda if something happens to me, just know that I love the both of you dearly," Sharnese said losing her breath. Her eyes rolled to the back of her head. She had never been so scared in her entire life. Big Ben pulled off to leave but was blocked by the paramedics that had arrived on the scene. Blood was steady seeping through Sharnese's gown as she hollered out in pain.

"Please get me some help," she said between breaths.

Destiny flagged down one of the EMTs that were passing by.

"Someone help us. My friend is pregnant, and she's losing a lot of blood," screamed Destiny.

The EMT quickly rushed over to the truck. She wasted no time putting on her rubber gloves. She grabbed a pair of scissors from out of the bag that she carried, and cut away at Sharnese's gown. When she pulled her dress up, she spoke into her two-way radio and called for backup.

"Ma'am, I'm a need for you to take a deep breath, and get ready to push for me. This baby will be here very soon."

Sharnese didn't want to deliver her baby in the backseat of the truck, but she didn't really have a choice.

"You two, grab a hold of her legs for me," she said to Murda and Money.

Money backed up while throwing his hands in the air. "Can't do it," he said. He and Murda had just had this conversation a few days ago, and besides, he didn't feel comfortable looking at his man's wife's private area.

"Move out of the way," Destiny said as she held open Sharnese's legs as far as she could get them.

"On the count of three push for me," the EMT said to Sharnese.

"Aarrgh," Sharnese hollered out as she pushed. The baby's head could be seen coming out. After three more big pushes, Sharnese and Murda welcomed a healthy baby boy into the world. Sharnese was rushed to the hospital immediately. She had lost a tremendous amount of blood while giving birth and needed a blood transfusion.

Murda went to get in the back of an ambulance but was stopped by one of the EMTs.

"Sir, you can't ride in here," said the older black woman.

"This is my wife and son you're transporting. I'll be damn if I can't go with them."

"It's policy sir, and that's that."

"Policy my ass. All this time you've spent arguing with me, could've been used to get her to the nearest hospital, ya think?" Murda said pushing past the woman as he stood next to Sharnese and their son.

The EMT that had helped deliver the baby wasted no time getting Sharnese transported.

*****

Beep! Beep! Beep!

It was like Deja vu when Sharnese heard those sounds. She was hooked up to an IV to help replenish her fluids. She had lost a lot of blood and was extremely dehydrated. She looked around and saw neither Murda nor Cortez Jr. She clearly remembered giving birth.

Sharnese was just about to hit the call button when a nurse rolled in Baby Cortez, and not too far behind them stood Murda. They had just come back from having the baby circumcised.

"Did everyone make it out okay?" Sharnese asked concerned about some of the guests at the wedding.

The nurse took Sharnese's temperature and checked the swelling in her feet. "I'll be back to check up on you later. Make sure you get plenty of rest and be sure to drink lots of water. Call us if you need little man to go to the nursery for a while," she said.

Murda waited until the nurse was completely out of the room before he spoke. He didn't know how Sharnese would react once he told her the news of her cousin's death. He grabbed her hand and kissed it gently. "Baby, I'm sorry, but Brooklyn didn't make it," he said.

Sharnese let out a terrifying scream. "No!" She screamed causing the nurse to rush back in.

"Is everything okay?" The nurse asked.

"Yes, she's fine. I just told her about a death in the family that's all." Murda reassured the nurse that everything was fine.

"I'm sorry for your loss sweetheart. Please take it easy."

"Thank you." Sharnese managed to say through her tears. She watched the door shut and continued with her questions.

"I know Brooklyn did a lot of evil to a lot of people, but I would never wish death on her. Those babies of hers are now motherless. Oh, my God. How is Money doing?" Sharnese said placing her hand over her mouth. She had totally forgotten about Money's relationship to Brooklyn.

"I can't call it. I haven't talked to him since we left," said Murda.

Her heart went out to Lil' Sincere. Out of Brooklyn's four kids, he was the youngest. She couldn't imagine the effect it would have on him. Losing a mother at any age was a hard pill to swallow, but Sharnese knew Destiny would do a wonderful job being a mother figure to him.

"Damn, I just can't believe she's gone," Sharnese said to Murda. Her heart was heavy. She and Brooklyn were very close growing up. She had shared so many secrets with her that it wasn't funny. Sharnese thought about the events that had taken place earlier and wondered how she went from being the happiest woman in the world to now feeling depressed and lost. Suddenly her whole attitude changed as she thought about the woman and her daughter who damn near ruined her wedding before it was actually ruined.

"That reminds me. Who the hell was that bitch that popped her ass up at the wedding claiming she has *a thirteen-year-old daughter with you?*" Sharnese asked as she emphasized the word thirteen.

Murda thought long and hard before he decided to tell Sharnese exactly who Journee was. He just hoped that Sharnese would remain the soldier she has been once he told her. "That was Journee," Murda replied looking down at the tile on the floor.

"Okay. Now, who the hell is Journee? And where the hell did she come from?" She asked. Her peace had been stolen for the day, so Murda wasn't about to have any either. She had questions that she wanted answers to, and she was determined to get them.

Murda cleared his throat and swallowed hard. He knew if he didn't tell Sharnese what she wanted to know, she would surely go off.

"Journee and I dated back in high school. One day she just up and moved away. Today was the first time I've seen her in years."

Sharnese could feel that Murda was telling the truth, but she felt like he was leaving something out on purpose.

"Where does this daughter stuff come into play?" She asked. "I mean, was she pregnant when she left?"

''I honestly don't know," Murda said. He wanted to know those same answers. For Journee's sake, he hoped that she wasn't just saying it to stir up some drama. Murda was far from the little boy that she knew back in high school.

"Let me be clear about this, so make sure you hear me, and hear me well. If by chance this child comes out to be yours then we will both take care of her. We will also be paying this Journee bitch a visit together," she said. Sharnese was hoping that Murda made an argument about them approaching Journee together, so she could go upside his head.

Murda simply replied, "No problem." He wasn't about to argue with her while she was still in the hospital.

"And Murda make this the last time I have to deal with your other bitches. My patience is growing thin, and you're threatening to bring out a side of me that you don't want to see."

Murda glared at Sharnese, but he didn't say a word. Had she had been anybody else he would've blown her head off for making such threats. He was ashamed to say that he was to blame for how she was acting. If he had been faithful from the beginning, Sharnese would not have had such ill feelings. The ink had barely dried on their marriage certificate and already he was on the verge of losing his wife.

After laying the law down to Murda, all Sharnese wanted to do was sleep. Her body was still sore from giving birth, and that mixed with the drama from the wedding was too much for her mind to consume. She pressed the button on the I.V. and waited for the pain medication to kick in. Baby Cortez had found his way back to the nursery. The nurses in there had fallen in love with him. Just that fast Murda was already in the spare bed fast asleep. Sharnese played around with the buttons on the remote trying to position the bed so that she could get comfortable. After minutes of fidgeting around, she finally found a spot that she could sleep in. Before she knew it, the medicine had begun to take its course, and it had her feeling woozy. Her eyes got real heavy as they closed shut for a temporary rest.

*****

One Week Later...

Sharnese, Destiny, Murda, and Money sat in the back of the black limo. Across from them sat Mama Peaches, Tony, Brooklyn's mother Jackie, and Brooklyn's children. After Jackie heard the news about her oldest daughter, she made it her business to stay clean and get her life on the right track.

Destiny took Money's hands and placed them on her lap. Money was trying his hardest to remain strong for his son. As much as he hated Brooklyn, he was hurt that her children had to experience such pain. They were too young to understand why their mother had gone to heaven.

Sharnese was surprised to see how many people were outside of the church, considering the fact that Brooklyn had so many enemies.

Once everyone was out of the limo, Murda grabbed Sharnese's hand as they were led down the aisle to the first pew. Mama Peaches felt her legs ready to give out. The sight of the white casket sickened her stomach. Too many times she had warned Brooklyn about the lifestyle she was living, and now here she was burying her granddaughter all because she didn't take heed of the warnings she had been given. Murda and Money caught her just in time as they helped her to her seat. Making sure she was alright, they took their seats next to their wives.

Sharnese's heart was beating rapidly. She wasn't ready to say her final farewells to her cousin. She refused to even look in the direction of the casket. Tears clouded her vision as she realized this would be their last time together.

Once everyone was seated, Pastor Mason began. "Family and friends, we are gathered here today, not to mourn, but to celebrate the life of Brooklyn Santana."

Not a dry eye was in the building once the pastor was done speaking. It was now time for the final viewing of Brooklyn's body. Sharnese was not ready to come to terms that Brooklyn was the one inside of the casket. The usher's escorted the family to the body. Sharnese stopped a few feet from the casket. She didn't feel like she could go on.

Murda turned to his side and saw the hesitation that was present in Sharnese's face. He grabbed a hold of her hand and whispered, "You can do this." He knew that Sharnese would have a hard time, considering how close she and Brooklyn had been. Murda was only there to support his wife and homeboy. He didn't give a fuck about Brooklyn. He couldn't get over the fact that Brooklyn damn near got their heads blown off with the reckless shit she had been doing. Some people would've called him heartless, but he didn't care. Had the shoe been on the other foot, they would've thought the same way. Hand in hand they stood in front of the casket. The funeral home had done a wonderful job fixing up her appearance. You couldn't even see the hole the bullet had implanted in her forehead.

Mama Peaches long cries could be heard from a mile away. To say she was devastated would be an understatement. Brooklyn looked like an angel who was resting peacefully. There was no way she was dead. The lifestyle Brooklyn lived no longer matter to Mama Peaches. The kids stood behind her waiting for their chance to say goodbye to their mother.

"Close it please," Mama Peaches said to the usher. She wasn't about to let the kids remember their mother in such a way. Although the makeup concealed the bullet wound, you could still see it, and this wasn't the time to explain to them how their mother lived her life. She wanted them to remember sweet memories they had with her.

Jackie shook her head in disagreement. She felt as if the kids should've been able to view their mother's body for the last time. Mama Peaches looked at her daughter with a look that said, "I dare you to say otherwise."

Bridgette I'esha

The usher did as she was told and granted Mama Peaches her wish. The family was no longer crying over Brooklyn's death. They wept for her children. It was time for them to come together and raise those kids as one. God had a reason for bringing them together under these circumstances. They had been away from each other for too long. Thirty minutes later Brooklyn was buried in the ground.

"Sleep peacefully baby girl," Sharnese said as she and the rest of the family let loose twenty-six white doves symbolizing the years Brooklyn had spent on this earth.

Mama Peaches walked over to Sharnese and hugged her tightly not wanting to let go. "Baby promise me that you'll help me guide these children in the right direction. I'm not asking you to take care of them, it's not your responsibility, but as a family, we need to stick together. All I'm asking you to do is help me with the things I won't be able to do. You know I'm getting up there in age," she said.

"You don't have to ask me to do such things," Sharnese said. She was more than willing to help Mama Peaches out when it came to the kids. None of Brooklyn's other kid's fathers even bothered to show up and pay their respects. They weren't even sure if they knew she was dead or not. Sharnese wanted to take in one of the kids and raise them in their home, but she needed to go over things with Murda first. They already had enough drama in their lives, and they didn't need anyone else getting killed.

"Thank you so much," she said kissing Sharnese on her cheek. No matter how old Sharnese got, she would always be Mama Peaches baby.

Once everyone was finished giving their condolences to the family, they all gathered back in the limo and went to Mama Peaches house where they ate, laughed, played cards and just reminisced about the good old times.

Chapter Fifteen

It was the wee hours of the night and Murda sat in front of the old run-down building Jermaine was hiding at waiting for Money. Murda had his trusty .357 in between his seat, and his .45 in the passenger seat beside him. The memories of Kas and Jermaine ruining his wedding haunted him in his head. He wouldn't be able to walk around freely until he killed him. With Kas out of the way, Murda still wasn't satisfied. He wanted everyone who played a part in the massacre that took place at his wedding to pay. Murda was just about to call Money when he heard a tap at his window. Money was dressed in his all black ready to put in work clothes. He made sure he had his gloves on his hands. He didn't need the police tracing back his fingerprints on anything. He wasn't about to get caught up in no murder charge. Money was always about being low-key when he committed a crime. He couldn't see himself going down for doing something dumb. Normally, they would've had ski-masks on too, but tonight they wanted Jermaine to see his killers before he met his maker.

Quietly they got out of the car and made their way along the side of the building. Murda had paid neighborhood crackhead twenty dollars to signal them if he saw or heard anyone coming. Money pressed his ear against the door and heard the sounds of slurping.

"Yo, this nigga in here getting his dick wet," Money said trying to muffle his chuckle.

"He better enjoy it. This will be his last time getting any pussy on this earth."

Murda stood back and kicked the door in taking it completely off its hinges. He was disgusted at the sight that stood before him. Big Ben's fat ass was on his knees sucking the life out of Jermaine's dick. All of these years he would've never thought that the man who he looked up to was a homo thug, and a traitor. Murda yanked his gun from out of his waist and aimed it at him.

"It's not what you think. Let me explain," Ben said pleading for his life.

"You're right it's not what I think. It's what I see. Ya, big grown ass sucking another's man dick like it ain't enough pussy in

Bridgette I'esha

the world. And if that ain't enough you're associating with the enemy. Something is clearly wrong with this picture.

POP! Murda let off a shot that landed in between Big Ben's legs. His penis was barely attached as he cried out in pain trying to hold together what very little was still there. His hands were covered in blood. It was a gruesome sight to see as the blood ran down the inside of his legs.

"Quit crying like a little bitch. Do you need something for the pain?" He asked.

The pain must have been unbearable for him because without thinking he replied, "Yes."

Ben had his eyes closed trying to block out the pain.

"Here, I got you a painkiller," Murda said to him.

Ben wasted no time opening his eyes. When he looked up, he was relieved of his pain.

POP, POP, POP! Murda sent three shots to his chest. He wanted Ben's death to be more crucial, but time wasn't on his side. He let off three more shots into his body as his anger took over him. He couldn't believe that the man he had trusted into his home had betrayed him in the worst way. He then started to wonder if Ben had been the one leaking information to them the entire time.

How could I have been so fucking stupid? He better hope I don't decide to go on a killing spree with his fucking family. I trusted him around my wife and my son. I can't believe this shit. Murda said to himself.

Jermaine got up to make a run for it. He knew if he didn't then he wouldn't be making it out of there alive. He was damn near out the door when he was met by the barrel of a gun pointing in his face.

"Just where the hell do you think you're going?" Asked Money. He liked to taunt his victims a little before their death.

Jermaine said nothing. Wasn't no point in trying to cop a plea, especially when he knew he was going to die anyway.

"You need to just go ahead it, and get it over with," he said poking his chest out trying to be tough when just a few seconds ago he was trying to run for his life

"Okay smartass, say hello to your maker," Money said blowing off Jermaine's entire face. Pieces of flesh landed on his shirt. It was time for him and Murda to go. They had been in there long enough. They didn't need any good Samaritans getting up investigating the sounds of the gunshots.

"Give me that gun so I can toss it over the bridge." Murda handed Money both guns he had on him. The state of New York did not play when it came to people owning guns without permits, especially minorities.

"Have Destiny call Sharnese so I can know that you made it home," Murda said peeling off the latex gloves that were still on his hands.

"Bet," Money replied.

Just like that, they disappeared out the door. The crackhead that Murda had paid was still there standing on the curb. Murda reached into his pocket and pulled out a fifty-dollar bill. Normally he wouldn't have given the man any more money, but he had really looked out for him.

"Take this and get out of here," Murda said shoving the money into the man's hand and dipping off into the night.

*****

Sharnese answered the door to see four FBI agents walking on her freshly cut lawn.

"Is there something I can help you gentlemen with this morning?" She asked wondering what the hell was going on.

An older white man with salt and pepper colored hair stepped forward. "We're looking for a Cortez Rodriguez," he said as he tried to get a peek inside of the house.

"Hold on for one minute please," she said. She called out Murda's government name. "Cortez." Only to be met with an angry face in return. Murda walked out of the kitchen eating a Turkey Club sandwich. His face was all tore up, but Sharnese didn't give a damn.

"Why the hell are you calling out my government like ya ass is the damn police. Are you working with them?" He asked trying to piece together what was going on.

"Sshh," she said with one finger placed against his lips. "The FBI is at the front door and they're asking for you."

Murda couldn't believe his ears. He was always so careful with everything he did. Since getting out of the game a few months ago, he hadn't had any dealings with the streets. He had finally settled down with the love of his life. He got up and went to the door.

"Cortez Rodriguez?" The agent asked

Bridgette I'esha

"Yeah, why?"

"You are under arrest for the murder of Natalie O'Neal."

Chapter Sixteen

"What do you mean he's under arrest for murder?" Sharnese asked playing dumb. She knew sooner or later the day would come when law enforcement showed up at their door.

"Unless you want to take a ride downtown with him I would recommend that you remain quiet." Sharnese wanted to say something back, but she didn't want to make things any worse.

"Get in the house and call my lawyer," Murda instructed her before he was hauled off. Immediately Sharnese called Destiny to inform her of what was going on. She cried like a baby when Destiny revealed that he would more than likely be in there until Monday. It was a weekend and no judges were available.

Sharnese sat by the phone waiting to hear from Murda. It had been a tough task trying to take care of the baby, run the salon, and meet with Destiny to discuss Murda's fate. Murda was looking at anywhere from twenty-five years to life. The judge had denied Murda's request for bail. The state of New York did not play when it came to law enforcement getting killed. The judge and the state's prosecutor considered Murda to be a flight risk.

"Sharnese will you relax over there. All that damn leg shaking you doing is making me nervous," Mama Peaches said as she rocked baby Cortez in her arms. She had been helping Sharnese with the baby while Murda was away. Mama Peaches felt that Sharnese could use all the help she could get. It wasn't easy being a first-time mom and Sharnese had a lot to learn.

"Mama Peaches I'm trying," Sharnese said checking her phone again. "I'm getting lovesick not being able to see him." Mama Peaches rolled her eyes at Sharnese's overdramatic ass. Murda had only been gone for two weeks, but to Sharnese it felt like a century.

"Whatever chile. He will call you. Just rest ya nerves like I said." As if Mama Peaches could read the future, Sharnese's phone sounded off playing Future's song *No Matter What*. She excused herself and went into her bedroom to take the call in private.

"You have a collect call from "Cortez" an inmate at Riker's Island Correctional Facility. To accept the charges, press one now. Otherwise press…" Sharnese didn't give the automatic system a chance to finish the rest of the recording before she began pressing one repeatedly. She pressed so hard she almost cracked the screen on her phone.

"Hey bae," Sharnese said happily into the phone. She missed hearing the sound of his voice.

"What's happening shawty?" Murda replied back. He hated talking on the phone in the jail. Everything you said was being recorded and could be used against you if necessary. He had to be careful about what he said to Sharnese over the phone.

"How's my little man?" Murda asked. The fact that he wasn't home being a father figure to his son was killing him. He didn't care that baby Cortez would never remember it, it was the fact that he would, which made him upset.

"Greedy as hell. Thank God, I'm breastfeeding or we would be buying formula every day. He's already holding his head up on his own. The doctor says he's advanced for his age already."

"Word! I'm ready to be reunited with the two of you. The crazy shit you gotta deal with in here is not for me. You always got that one nigga who wants to try you," Murda said eyeing some dude that kept walking back and forth by the telephones.

"Cortez, please tell me you haven't done anything that will get you into more trouble?" Sharnese asked. She knew Murda's attitude could get the best of him and fog his judgment. She didn't need him doing anything that would keep him in there any longer.

"Nese, I had to let these niggas know that my hands are official. Of course, I had some young niggas who caught wind of who I was and they beat dude's brains loose. But enough of all that." Murda realized he had said too much as it was. "But check this out, Saturday I'm a need you to take that ride and come visit me, but leave the baby at home."

"Okay, but why?" Sharnese asked not understanding why Murda didn't want to see their son.

"This isn't a place where I want to be spending time with my son. It's bad enough I'm asking you to come up here," Murda said growing agitated with Sharnese questioning him.

"I guess I can make that happen," Sharnese said with an attitude.

"I'm not asking you! I'm telling you Sharnese. Damn, I got enough I'm dealing with as it is. I don't need all the extra shit you giving a nigga."

"Damn, my bad! You ain't got to cop a fucking attitude," Sharnese replied back. She wasn't feeling Murda's attitude tonight. She just wanted him to see his son.

Murda felt bad for taking his frustrations out on Sharnese. It wasn't her fault that he was behind bars. He was just asking for her to follow his lead. "Look ma, I apologize for getting all hostile and shit," Murda said apologizing. As a child, his father had taught him that saying sorry meant you really didn't mean it. But saying that you apologized meant you were being sincere and speaking from the heart. Murda took a few minutes to reflect back on what had got him there. Thinking with his dick had damn near cost him his life. Natalie was dead and here she was still harassing him. With all the witnesses in attendance at the church, he knew it would be impossible for his charges to hold up against him in court. Big Jimmy was even trying to pull some strings to have him released on bond.

"I guess I accept your apology," Sharnese smiled like Murda could see it through the phone. She could never stay mad at him for too long. They had been through hell and high waters, so the petty argument that they were having was nothing. Sharnese relationship with Murda was far from perfect. Things hadn't always been the way she expected them to be between the two of them, but she was willing to ride with him until the end.

"You have five minutes remaining," the operator reminded them.

"Have I had any visitors?" Murda said beating around the bush. He wanted to come straight out and ask if Journee had visited the house, but he didn't want to piss Sharnese off by asking about another woman. He had yet to figure out why she decided to come back to town. He hadn't seen her since his high school years and now she was claiming he had fathered her daughter. Everything about the situation sounded fishy to him. He didn't know whether he should just ignore the accusations or do some investigating of his own. Either way, he needed to find out what she had up her sleeve.

"Unless they came while I was out running errands then I don't think so. I'll have to ask Mama Peaches about that since she's the one here during the day," Sharnese said not catching on to what Murda was asking.

"Nah, you ain't got to go through all that. If they need to see me that bad they know where to reach me at. But look this phone is ready to hang up on us at any second, kiss the baby for me and just have ya pretty ass down here come this weekend. If you can't make it then cool, I understand."

"There's no mountain in this world high enough that will stop me from getting to you. I love you, Cortez."

"I love you too, Sharnese," Murda managed to say before the line went dead. When he hung the phone up the same dude that had been walking past him earlier was doing it again.

"You the Murda that run with Money?" the man named Chico asked as he approached Murda.

"Yeah what's up?" Murda said getting into a fighting a stance. He didn't know this man for him to be asking about him, but he was willing to make an example out of him too if necessary. Chico threw his hands up to surrender. He wasn't coming at Murda on no bullshit. He needed to discuss some business opportunities with him and put him up on game about Rich.

"I come in peace my brotha."

"What's good then?" Murda asked. He didn't know this man for him to be coming at him period. He just wanted to do whatever time he was gonna do and go home.

"That nigga Rich that ya young boy Pop run with been going around town talking real reckless about you." Murda looked around to see if anyone was ear hustling on their conversation. Everyone was tuned into the Nick Minaj's *Anaconda* music video. He shook his head at the grown men growing excited over nothing.

"Follow me," Murda said to Chico. His curiosity was getting the best of him. He wanted to see if the information the man was about to present to him was valuable. Too many times he told Money he felt something about Rich wasn't right. Since passing everything down to Pop, he and Money didn't feel the need to interfere with the drug game. They could only pass their knowledge down, but they couldn't force him to use it. Once inside his cell, Murda instructed Chico to take a seat on the bottom bunk.

"Have a seat," Murda said nodding his head towards the bunk. He had been lucky enough to not have a cellmate.

"I'd rather stand," Chico said feeling slightly uncomfortable. Murda's demeanor was enough to intimidate any man. He kept a straight face and showed very little emotion when speaking.

"I was telling you, not asking you," Murda said nodding his head again. This time Chico went ahead and sat down. He was beginning to wonder if approaching Murda about Rich was the right thing to do. He just hoped everything he planned on telling didn't backfire on him.

"Go ahead and finish. Your time in here is limited."

"One day I just happened to be in the barbershop while Rich was in there and he was talking out the side of his neck. He kept saying some shit about how easy it would be to take over the throne since you and Money had passed everything down to Pop. He kept talking about how Pop didn't know what he was doing and I could've sworn he said something about taking a trip down to Jamaica I believe so that he could meet the connect. He called his name but I can't quite call it, but I do remember it sounding like a Spanish name."

That was all Murda needed to hear. Everything that Chico had just said to him seemed to be true. And it could've only come from the source itself. There were only three people who knew the connect and it consisted of himself, Money, and Pop. So, the only way Rich could've known anything would've been if Pop told him. Something had to be done about Rich, but Murda sort of felt like it was no longer his concern since he wasn't in the drug game anymore.

"Good looking my man," Murda said smacking Chico on the back. "I'll be sure to tell my people to place some money on ya books this week."

"Thanks, man. I never did like that nigga Rich anyway. He always seemed like some kind of snake to me." Murda was just about to reply when the sound of sirens started going off throughout the building. A fight had broken out somewhere, so everybody had to return to their cells immediately.

"I'll get up with you later," Chico said as he exited the cell.

Murda laid down on his bunk and stared at the ceiling. He didn't know what he was going to do with the new problem at hand. Although he wanted no parts in the matter, he knew it would be impossible once Money got involved. It seemed like every time he turned around some kind of drama was always headed his way. He was starting to wonder if it was even possible to leave the game behind.

*****

Sharnese stood at the window in the kitchen washing dishes. Although they had a dishwasher Sharnese preferred to hand wash their dishes. Cleaning allowed her to have a peace of mind. It was crazy how the things she hated doing as a child she didn't mind now. The glow from the stars captivated her attention. It was the simple things that she enjoyed the most. She had encountered so many life-changing situations over the last year, she was rarely given time to herself.

Sharnese closed her eyes as she allowed her mind to take her on a trip down memory lane. Her deceased cousin Brooklyn had been on her mind heavy. It had only been a month since she had been buried in the ground. Many people felt at ease with Brooklyn being out of the picture. She had destroyed so many people lives with the lies she told. Most of the people that showed up to her funeral had only gone to see if she was really dead. You could only believe half of what you heard and only what you saw. Once it was confirmed that Brooklyn was indeed dead, some of her enemies got together and had a full block party to celebrate her death. It was crazy how far people would go nowadays.

Sharnese's quiet time was interrupted when the doorbell rang. She wasn't expecting any visitors this time of night. She took off the apron she was wearing and went to answer the door. She damn near lost her mind when she found Journee standing on her front step.

Bridgette I'esha

"I know you tripping now bringing ya ass to my house," Sharnese said causing a commotion which sent Mama Peaches flying down the stairs.

"Bitch please, I'm not here to see you," Journee said being disrespectful. "Now where is Murda?" Sharnese couldn't believe that Journee was bold enough to bring drama to her house. Sharnese was trying hard to keep her composure. Journee had almost ruined her wedding trying to confess her love for Murda. Now she was popping her ass up at the place they rested their heads, which was the ultimate sign of disrespect.

"I wouldn't give a damn if you were here to see President Obama! You need to leave before shit gets real," Sharnese said as she took a step closer to Journee. She showed no signs of fear or intimidation. She was going to get her point across one way or another. She was tired of being the quiet Sharnese that everybody thought they could just run over top of. Majority of the time she carried herself with class, but this Journee chick was really testing her gangster.

Journee laughed at Sharnese like she was a joke. She had heard from her first cousin Monique that Sharnese wasn't about that life. But what Monique failed to mention was that Sharnese was the reason she had that nasty cut alongside her face. Journee had no idea that her cousin was setting her up for failure. Journee took her finger and poked Sharnese in the middle of her forehead. It would be the last touch she would get before Sharnese went to work on her ass.

"Bitch, don't you ever in your life put ya fucking hands on me," Sharnese said sending straight shots to Journee's head. Mama Peaches started to break up the fight but instead, she stood back and watched her granddaughter defend herself. She was proud of Sharnese for standing her ground. Sharnese was normally the quiet one who tended to stay out of drama. But it was also the quiet ones who could do the most damage. Sharnese showed Journee no mercy as she continued to throw her hands like she was a heavyweight champion in a boxing match. Through all the hits Journee received, she still continued to talk her shit.

"One thing about me, I don't give a fuck about Cortez being your husband. I don't mind breaking up happy homes or sharing a nigga if that's what it takes to make me or my daughter happy. I'll do whatever is necessary to get what I want," Journee said with a bloody mouth.

"What's mine shall always be mine and I'll fight till the death of me to prove that. Now listen, and listen well while I make myself clear. Make this your first and last time bringing ya ratchet ass on my property. You do see there's a no trespassing sign right there in my window," Sharnese said point to the sign that was easily visible at night since it glowed.

"Every time we see each other in public you better hope and pray that our son isn't with me cause bitch I'm going to work on ya ass. I don't care if we at the grocery store, the bank or the church, you best to believe it's going down! Now get ya dusty ass on somewhere," Sharnese said. Sharnese took her foot and kicked Journee square up her ass just as she tried to get up from off the ground. "Bitch you ain't moving fast enough," Sharnese said again hoping Journee tried to do something stupid. Journee got to her car and pulled her pants down exposing her bare ass. The nasty heifer didn't even have on any panties.

"You can eat this cake and kiss my entire ass. I hope Cortez's dick is still good like it was years ago," Journee said as she stood in front of her car. It was obvious the ass whipping Sharnese gave her didn't mean much to her as she was steady running her mouth...but from a distance.

Sharnese went inside the house while Journee kept on yelling all types of obscenities. Sharnese smiled when she saw her tote, which held her best friend. She kissed the tip of the chrome Magnum .45 before going back outside. She hid the gun behind her back and just listened to every foul word that came out of Journee's mouth. Finally growing tired of her mouth, Sharnese released a warning shot into the air. It was enough to make Journee quieter than a church mouse. She hauled ass trying to get away from the gunfire. Sharnese aimed the gun in the direction of Journee just for the hell of it. Murda's side bitches were going to start respecting her one way or another. Journee backed out the driveway and got ghost. She had left Armani unattended at the hotel. She was only supposed to be going out to get them some food. Instead, she went looking for trouble and found just that.

Bridgette I'esha

Sharnese grabbed her phone from off the counter and dialed Destiny's number. She needed to find out every piece of information known about Journee. Sharnese wanted to have the upper hand on her. She was willing to go as far as hiring a private investigator if it came down to it.

"What's up Nese?" Destiny answered in a jolly mood.

"I need you to find out all the information you can on that bitch Journee," Sharnese said pacing the floor. She was still amped up from her confrontation with Journee so sleep was the last thing on her mind.

"Why does that name sound so familiar?"

"How could you forget the bitch that damn near ruined my wedding day?"

"Okay, yeah her. Do I need to put my combat boots on and go to war?" asked Destiny.

Sharnese loved that Destiny always had her back. They didn't need to have conversations every day to define their friendship. Their friendship had been in their hearts since the first day they met. They both had cried on each other's shoulders at one point in time.

"I done went to war and back in the last twenty minutes. That bitch had the nerve to bring her ass over here. Got me fighting on my front lawn and letting shots off in the air like I don't live around these damn white folks," Sharnese said huffing and puffing. She was getting mad all over again. She was upset with herself for letting Journee even get her out of character like that. Sometimes Sharnese tends to forget that she was the wife of a boss and she needed to carry herself in the same manner. She knew Murda would not be pleased to hear about his wife fighting. But what was she supposed to do? She had been put in a situation where she had no choice but to stand her ground.

"What in the hell happened for you to go off like that?" Destiny asked knowing it took a lot to get on Sharnese's bad side. Sharnese was the type that kept to herself. Her main goal was getting money and thinking of ways to get more. She hadn't even told anyone that she was working on her own clothing line. She wanted to wait until everything was official before she went ahead and announced it. People would congratulate you and still be praying for your downfall. Sharnese wasn't trying to curse her blessing before it even happened.

"She was being disrespectful as hell. Talking about she wanted Murda back and she didn't mind breaking up homes. But can you believe this nasty ass bitch pulled down her pants and told me to kiss her ass though? That's what made me go and get my good ol friend Mr. Chrome."

Destiny was in tears when Sharnese finished telling her story. As hard as she tried, she just couldn't imagine Sharnese going that hard in front of Mama Peaches. She didn't know where this new Sharnese had come from, but she needed to keep her around.

"Are you gonna help a friend out or not?" Sharnese asked.

"Don't worry boo, I got you. I can't have you sitting in jail too."

"How is his case coming along?" Sharnese asked hoping Destiny would tell her more than Murda did.

"Have you talked to your husband?" Destiny asked. Sharnese was her best friend, but she didn't feel comfortable disclosing her client's information without his consent. If Murda wasn't telling Sharnese too much then she was sure it was for a good reason. Destiny tried not to let her business and personal life intervene with one another.

"Yeah, but he didn't say much of nothing. He had a little attitude when I talked to him earlier."

"Just about every man that's locked down tend to have attitudes. Trust me, if don't nobody else know I do. Some of the clients I deal with be making me want to say to hell with defending their asses, but I just brush that shit off to the side. But look it's getting late and just like I have to get up in the morning, so do you."

"Yeah, you're right. I'm tired as hell now. Call me when you get some free time tomorrow," Sharnese said yawning into the phone.

"Okay girl bye."

They both ended the call and prepared for tomorrow's workday. It was just the beginning of the week and they had a long way to go before they reached Friday.

Chapter Seventeen

Sharnese woke up the next morning with a horrible headache and bags underneath her eyes. She didn't get much sleep the night before. She had been up-all-night thinking of ways to get rid of Journee. She understood that if Journee's daughter Armani was indeed Murda's that the two of them would have to co-parent which was fine with her. She would never stop Murda from being a father to his daughter, but she would, however, make sure all of their gatherings took place in public. Sharnese was a woman herself and she knew women would do the extreme to get what they wanted.

Sharnese got out of the bed and went to go do her daily morning routine. Once she was done showering and applying her cosmetics, she placed a few loose curls in her hair. It was crazy how she did hair for a living, yet she hated to do her own. It was a little before seven thirty and the salon didn't open until nine, so she decided to take the extra weight off Mama Peaches by making everyone breakfast. It was tough on Mama Peaches; she had been awarded full custody of Brooklyn's oldest son Jordan since his father never stepped forward. Mama Peaches refused to see the family split apart, so she took it upon herself to give the child a good life. Despite Brooklyn not being too much of a mother, Jordan showed Mama Peaches the utmost respect. He never got slick out the mouth like most children and she didn't have to stay on him about cleaning up after himself. He listened and he only spoke when he was spoken to. Mama Peaches made it her business to get all of Brooklyn's children at least one weekend out of the month. She made sure to tell them to stick together no matter what when they were all around each other. Family meant a lot to Mama Peaches and she wanted the kids to feel the same way.

Sharnese grabbed the salon smock from off the bed and went downstairs. To her surprise, Mama Peaches was already throwing down in the kitchen. The smell of the maple flavored bacon made Sharnese's mouth water. She had been on a strict diet since having the baby, but she was coming really close to giving in. Mama

Peaches was rinsing off the last of the potatoes when she felt someone standing behind her.

"Good morning Mama Peaches," Sharnese said as she fixed herself a French vanilla latte. Murda had gotten her a Keurig machine as a wedding gift and it was the best thing he could've ever brought her. It could be a hundred degrees outside and she still had to have a latte or cappuccino. She couldn't stand the smell or taste of coffee.

"Good morning baby. How are you feeling this morning?" Mama Peaches said as she put the potatoes into an iron skillet along with some onions. Sharnese knew then she would be losing the battle to stick with her diet.

"I'm fine," Sharnese replied. She wasn't in the mood to discuss the events that took place the night before. Once Mama Peaches mouth got to running it would be damn near impossible to shut her up.

"I'm just glad you stood up for yourself. That girl overstepped her boundaries by coming to your house. She was beyond disrespectful and I wanted to give her one of Mama Peaches old school ass whippings," Mama Peaches said as she thought back to her younger days as a Madam. She didn't tolerate any form of disrespect, especially not over no man. It was one thing to have drama with another woman in the streets, but once you got bold and brought it to their front door, then in her eyes you deserved everything that came your way.

"Can we not do this? It's too early. I don't even want to think about that broad," Sharnese turned on the morning news. She loved to keep up with the current events, but she was really checking to see if Murda's case made the headlines. The media was so concerned with Natalie being an active member of law enforcement, but they failed to mention the fact that she had several open cases of stalking before her death.

Sharnese was glad that she had encouraged Murda to keep all of the threatening messages Natalie had sent to his phone. She even had witnesses from the wedding who didn't mind testifying on

Murda's behalf. The media was making Murda out to be a menace to society, claiming that he killed Natalie because he had a strong hatred towards the law. Sharnese found it quite amusing how they didn't once mention any of the good things he did for the community. Prior to Murda getting arrested, he had just donated shoes and coats to the school system. Winter was right around the corner and he wanted every child to be protected from the brutal winter weather. Finally hearing enough bad talk about her husband, Sharnese shut the television off. Mama Peaches placed a plate of food on the table in front of her. Sharnese attempted to push it off to the side, but Mama Peaches wasn't having it.

"Chile, don't play with me. You gonna sit there and eat this here good food. Here I done slaved over this hot stove."

Reluctantly, Sharnese went ahead and took a few bites of the food. She was in no mood to argue with Mama Peaches. She just wanted some peace before she went to the salon. She thanked Mama Peaches for the meal and went upstairs to the nursery to check on her little man. She wouldn't be able to function throughout the day if she didn't see him before she left the house. Even with him being in the care of Mama Peaches, she still made it a habit to call home every hour.

$$$$$$$$$$$

Sharnese noticed a few of her employees standing outside of the salon which was unusual for a Monday morning. Normally everyone would've been inside getting things situated for the day. Sharnese walked through the front door and her heart dropped. Someone had vandalized the entire salon. The word bitch had been spray painted at all the stations. They even went as far as shattering all the mirrors in the salon. The only thing they didn't manage to destroy was her office. It was impossible for them to get inside with knowing the correct passcode, along with having the key.

"Has anyone filed a police report?" Sharnese asked her employees, hoping that they hadn't. She had a strong feeling Journee was behind the destruction of her business. It was too much of a coincidence that someone had destroyed her property the day after their altercation.

"No, we were waiting until we heard from you," said Shawna, another hairstylist that worked in the salon.

"Thank you. I deeply apologize for this messing up the flow of everyone's money. From the damage that has been done, we're looking at the salon being shut down for at least a week."

Everyone let out a few grunts. Nobody liked for their money to be messed with. Sharnese understood that everyone had kids to take care of and bills that needed to be paid so she told everyone not to worry about their booth rent and she would reimburse them for any appointments that they had to cancel. She understood that everyone didn't have the proper tools to do hair from out of their homes. Besides, some of the people who worked in the salon were really funny about people knowing where they lived and she couldn't blame them. It was always the person you least expected that would rob you in a second. All of the stylists in the salon charged a pretty good penny for their services, but they had the skills to match the prices. You could walk into Sharnese's salon and get a hairstyle that you wouldn't see anywhere else. Sharnese hadn't even told them that she was thinking about entering the shop into a beauty contest. She wanted to show the world the craft that they all had been blessed with. They were all talented and hustled hard.

From the very beginning, Sharnese had let each of them know that anything other than professionalism would not be tolerated. Unlike most salons, there was no competition amongst the stylists; if anything, they helped each other master their craft. They were all family and she expected everyone to act as a team.

"Thank you, Shawna," Sharnese said stepping over pieces of glass. It hurt her to see everything she worked so hard for go down the drain. Sharnese could have given up but instead, she looked at it as motivation to go harder. It was obvious someone was a tad bit envious of her accomplishments. To her, it would be nothing more than an early upgrade to the salon. If they were mad now, then they would only shit bricks once everything was complete.

"Everybody can go ahead and take the rest of the week off. Don't worry about this month's booth rent. I got everybody covered."

"Now boss lady, you know we aren't going to leave you to clean up this mess by yourself," Shawna said speaking for everybody. It shocked Sharnese considering the fact that she was usually quiet. Everyone gathered into groups as they cleaned up the mess.

Sharnese went inside her office to view the surveillance camera. All the proof she needed was right there on the videotape. Journee was indeed behind it all. Sharnese studied the tape some more, but couldn't make out who her accomplice was. Sharnese got on the phone and called the insurance company. They informed her that they wouldn't be able to do anything until a police report was filed. She really didn't want to get the police involved but she wasn't trying to spend unnecessary money if she didn't have to. It was no telling how long Murda would be locked up. She wanted to be able to take care of their son and manage all the bills, with or without him being there.

After turning everything over to the police, they assured her that everything would be handled in a timely manner. Once the salon was cleaned up, Shawna helped Sharnese pick out new decor for the salon. Sharnese had to give Shawna her props, just like her Shawna had good taste and she knew her shit.

$$$$$$$$$$

The drama from the last few days had left Sharnese feeling drained and exhausted. Sharnese wanted to do nothing more than to go home and have a drink. She was in denial about her turning into an alcoholic like her mother had been. The only difference was Sharnese didn't drink to get rid of her problems, she just liked the feeling it gave her on the inside.

On the way home, she stopped by a local liquor store. She needed some Patron and Tequila in her life. She was just about to pay for her merchandise when a voice from behind her told the cashier he had it. Sharnese turned around to see Pop standing there with his arms wide open. She hadn't seen him since the wedding.

His visits to the house had become less frequent since Murda had been gone.

"Pop baby! Where have you been?" Sharnese said like the two of them were long lost, friends.

"Shit, I've been laying low, getting this money. That's about it."

"Ain't nothing wrong with that." Sharnese moved off to the side so that the other customers in line could pay for their items. A couple of them caught attitudes but she paid them no mind as she and Pop went outside to finish their conversation in the parking lot.

"How's big homie's case coming along?" Pop asked. He wanted to pay Murda a visit, but he didn't want to draw any unwanted attention to the two of them. Pop was trying to stay off their radar. He was more than positive that the Feds were watching anybody that was affiliated with Murda.

"To be honest, I can't call it. Murda doesn't say too much over the phone. Hopefully, he'll have some good news to tell me during our upcoming visit."

"That's what's up. Be sure to tell him I asked for him. If I could, I would go and see him myself. But considering the circumstances, its best I leave well enough alone."

Pop turned off the alarm on his seven series Benz. Sharnese wanted to tell him he was doing too much, but it wasn't any of her business. You couldn't tell a grown man what to do. Sharnese took in every detail of the candy apple colored car. What caught her eye the most was the license plate. Pop had outdone himself with that one. Not only did the tag read BOSS with dollar signs next to it, but it was boarded in fucking diamonds. Pop was asking for somebody to rob him, or even worse, kill him. Sharnese could tell that Pop's new status in the streets was going to his head. He was being careless and in the end, it would cost him a terrible price. Sharnese had known Pop to be humble. He's smarter than what he was acting. Money was changing him and he didn't even realize he was putting everyone associated with him in danger. Sharnese and Pop said their goodbyes as they went their separate ways. Sharnese had made up her mind to fill Murda in on everything that was going on.

$$\$\$\$\$\$\$\$\$\$$

Five days later...

Saturday had come quicker than Sharnese had expected. She had tried on at least ten different outfits, trying to find the perfect one. She hadn't seen her husband in almost a month and she wanted to show him what it was he was missing. In the end, she decided on a pink long sleeve shirt, some white jeans, and a pair of pink and white retro Jordan's. Retro's were the only ones she wore. Sharnese made sure her jeans weren't too tight and that her shirt wasn't revealing. The security guards could be a trip when they wanted to, especially the females. Sharnese only had a couple of minutes before she needed to leave the house.

The bus ride over to visit Murda had Sharnese beyond irritated. The smell of cheap perfume and musk filled the overcrowded bus. The cries and screams from the unruly children made it no better. *This can't be life,* Sharnese thought to herself. She couldn't see how females made it an obligation to visit the jail every week; some went as much as three times a week. Sharnese turned her nose up at one of the females sitting beside her. There was a foul fishy smell coming from one of them. That alone set her attitude off even more. Riding on a dirty ass jail bus was beneath her. She shook her head as she listened to the several stories that the girls told about their men. One girl had the nerve to be bragging about how she would take her boyfriend's charge if it was going to reduce his sentence or get him off completely. Sharnese smirked a little as she listened to the big-boned light skin chick carry on with her conversation. She knew a real nigga would never put his woman in that type of position. She continued to ear hustle as she hoped this would be the first and last visit she would have to make.

It was a bittersweet moment for Sharnese as the bus approached the barb wired gates. Once inside of the facility, everyone was escorted to the security guards so that they and their belongings could be searched. Sharnese felt violated while she was searched roughly by one of the female correctional officers.

"Miss, you have entirely too much jewelry on for your visit," the woman said looking at the visitation sheet to see who it was Sharnese was there to visit. Emily the correctional officer shouted something out in Spanish to the other Spanish officer. They both fell out in laughter while Sharnese sat there with a dumbfounded look on her face. Emily had her eyes set on Murda since the first day he arrived there. She had tried everything that she could think of to seduce Murda, but it didn't work. She would put money on his books anonymously, but she was pretty sure he knew it was her. During chow time she made sure his cell was the last one to be opened. She wanted to have as much alone time with him as she could get.

"You're going to have to take something off and put it in a locker," Emily said as she threw a clear plastic bag down at Sharnese's foot.

Sharnese bit the inside of her jaw to stop herself from popping off slick. She wasn't about to fuck up her visit with Murda after traveling out this far out.

"Do I need to take off all my jewelry?" Sharnese asked, the line behind her was long and she didn't have the patience to be running back and forth.

"Did I say you needed to take everything off?" Emily said getting smart with Sharnese for the second time.

Sharnese didn't respond as she walked back out the doors to the locker room. To be on the safe side, she went ahead and removed all of her jewelry, except her wedding ring. She wasn't about to remove her symbol of love for nobody. Taking her time, Sharnese finally made it back to the line. Everything was running smoothly until she reached the end. Apparently, it was time for a random drug search. Out came the K9 dog and several more correctional officers. The dog sniffed around the entire room before stopping at Sharnese. The dog continued to bark and growl furiously at Sharnese.

"Ma'am come this way," one of the officers said while leading her to an empty room where she was instructed to get undressed as they prepared for a strip search.

"Why am I in here?" asked Sharnese.

"Apparently the K9 dog detected some kind of narcotics on you, which I'm not saying that you do, it's just the procedure."

Sharnese took off her clothes and showed them what they wanted to see. As she suspected, nothing was found and she was finally on her way back to see Murda. Sharnese sat at the table with butterflies in her stomach as she waited for the love of her life. Never in a million years did she imagine she would be in this predicament. Often, she would look down on people who were locked up, without knowing their situation. Now Murda was no saint, but Sharnese felt that everything he did was justified. She still didn't know every aspect of the game, but she knew enough to know nothing was off limits when it came to protecting yourself or your loved ones.

The sounds of the gates opening made her stomach even queasier. She was acting like this was the first time meeting him. When all of the inmates walked out except Murda, Sharnese began to worry. Several more minutes passed before Murda was escorted out by the same officer that had given her a hard time. Sharnese stood up as she waited for Murda to approach her. Sharnese was trying to figure out what the holdup was. Murda had been in the visiting room for at least ten minutes and he still hadn't made his way over to her. Sharnese saw an inmate sitting a nearby table with who she assumed was his girlfriend and decided to ask a few questions. This jail visit shit was still new to her so she figured there was something she was missing.

"Excuse me," Sharnese said as she walked over to the next table. "Is it normal to take this long before an inmate starts their visit?" The man and his girlfriend both turned their heads into the direction of the gates.

"I thought that bitch was banned from handling visits?" the girl said rolling her eyes. It was evident that the two had some type of altercation before.

"Is it that bad?" Sharnese asked, wanting to know all the scoop on the ignorant correctional officer.

"Honey, let me tell you. I had to check that bitch on several visits. Every time I come here she always bitching about me having on too much jewelry or that my clothes are too tight."

"That's the same shit she tried with me earlier."

All it is, she more than likely wanna fuck ya man and he done turned her swamp ass down. She ain't nothing but a thirsty bitch. I'm just surprised that she hasn't been fired yet. She already got kids by a couple of the inmates. She goes after any man who has some type of street reputation or money."

"Well damn, she gonna mess around and get fucked up for messing with somebody's man." Sharnese kept a straight face as she continued her conversation. Hearing how Emily got down had her feeling a little insecure. Murda had cheated before and she hoped he was smart enough to avoid anymore fuck ups. Murda had Sharnese looking like a fool once before and she refused to be played again. She wasn't sure if their relationship could last through any more hardships. They were still newlyweds, but Sharnese had no problem marching down to the courthouse and filing for an annulment.

"Ya hair is slayed! I might need to make an appointment with ya hairstylist," Sharnese looked at the weave in the girl's hair. It was nice, but it was nowhere near on the same level as Sharnese's skills.

"Thanks, you'll just have to come visit my salon so I can get you right. I'm Sharnese by the way."

"I'm Nicety," she responded back.

"I'm located right downtown. The shop is currently going through some renovations right now, but I do make home visits." Sharnese could tell that either Nicety or her man had money. The Prada heels she had on spoke for itself. Sharnese and Nicety were so wrapped up in their conversation the feeling of arms around her waist startled her and made her jump. Murda pulled Sharnese into his arms. It felt good to be in his arms, even if it was only for a few minutes.

"What's happening Chico?" Murda said as he nodded his head at Chico's ol lady. He wasn't about to have Sharnese chew his head off for speaking to another female.

"Ain't shit," Chico responded. "Still in this shit hole."

"Yeah, I feel you on that."

"Nicety, it was nice meeting you. We'll have to exchange information before we leave," Sharnese said running her hands up and down Murda's muscular arms. He had put on some muscle weight since he had been in there, his body was real buff.

"Most certainly," Nicety said while staring a hole in Emily as she walked over to their table.

"Rodriguez, have a seat now or you will be sent back to your cell."

Murda was growing tired of Emily harassing him. Ever since he had declined to have sex with her, she was always fucking with him. Murda had heard the many of stories about Emily; plain and simple she was a nasty bitch. There wasn't a nigga on his tier who hadn't been up inside of her raw, and he wanted no parts of that.

"Come on Nese before I fuck around and snap in this muthafucka." Murda and Sharnese walked back to the table hand in hand.

"Sit directly across from me and don't say nothing until this bitch is out of sight," Murda instructed Sharnese.

Sharnese did as she was told and remained quiet. But as soon as Emily was gone she started in with the questions, and she wasn't pulling off his ass. "What the fuck was that all about?" Sharnese questioned him. She spoke in a low tone, but loud enough for Murda to hear every word she was saying. "Let me guess, you done stuck ya dick inside of her too?" Sharnese said no longer able to control her emotions.

Murda shook his head. He was not in the mood to deal with the dumb shit from Sharnese today. He just wanted to have a nice visit and get caught up on anything he may have been missing at home. He knew he had fucked up several times before, but he was hoping they could get past that.

"Have I fucked shawty? No. Do I want to fuck her? No. Has she tried to give me some pussy? Yes. Worrying about another bitch is the least of my worries right now. The only thing I'm focused on is coming home to you." Sharnese blinked her eyes a couple of times to stop her tears from falling.

"Talk to me Nese, what's going on?"

"Everything is stressing me out. It's hard not having you home with us. It's enough dealing with ya baby mama drama."

"What baby mama drama?" Murda asked like he had no clue as to what Sharnese was talking about.

"Don't act like you don't remember the bitch that popped up unannounced at our wedding. You know the one who claims you're the father of her daughter. The child that looks exactly like you," Sharnese said trying to refresh his memory. Murda playing dumb had Sharnese's blood boiling on the inside. If they weren't in the jail, more than likely she would've gone upside his head for playing mind games.

Murda had really forgotten all about that situation with Journee, and to be honest, he was in no rush to deal with the drama. His problems concerning his case would be dealt with first. Earlier that morning he had spoken with Destiny and she informed him that the State's Attorney had until the middle of next week to present some evidence that made him guilty or he would be walking out of Riker's Island as a free man. Murda wasn't going to tell Sharnese though. He wanted it to be a surprise. He wanted to test her loyal grounds some more. She had already proven herself worthy, but a nigga could never be too sure when it came to females. Women were the sneakiest of them all. They could be sleeping with the enemy the entire time and you would never know. Women were discreet when they did their dirt. They didn't go around telling the world. Majority of them only got caught because they fucked with niggas who ran their mouths like bitches. Murda believed in the saying "*Out of sight, out of mind*" but it was mainly because he had gotten caught up one too many times.

"What drama have you had with her?" Murda asked Sharnese. It was obvious he was pissed off.

"Well for starters, she came to our house which resulted in me beating her ass on our front lawn. Then to top it off, the next morning I get to work and the entire salon had been vandalized. I mean everything in the salon had been destroyed. Glass was everywhere along with the word bitch."

To say Murda was mad would've been an understatement. He didn't know what type of games Journee was playing, but he was about to put an end to them. Everyone knew how protective Murda was when it came to Sharnese. He wasn't about to tolerate anybody disrespecting his wife. Murda couldn't win for losing when it came to the drama he had with women. It was enough to drive any sane man crazy. Murda didn't know how to make this situation right when he hadn't done anything wrong in the first place.

"I'll be right back," Sharnese said as she excused herself to use the bathroom. She was breaking down in a place where everybody was watching her. She took a wet paper towel and lightly dabbed away any of her makeup that had dripped. Sharnese gave herself a little pep talk in the mirror. *Get it together Sharnese. This is not the time to be getting all in your feelings. You got bitches out there waiting for you to fall off your game so that they can replace you,* she said out loud to herself. She walked out of the bathroom like the boss bitch she was. She put their personal life to the side for a minute. They would deal with those problems once Murda was released. Just that quick she had transformed into the Sharnese that he knew. Sharnese looked around to see if anybody was watching or listening to their conversation. Once she was sure that the coast was clear, she got down to business.

"On the real when you come home, you should sit down and have a talk with ya young boy."

"Let me guess, you are talking about Pop?" Murda asked for verification.

"Yeah, how you know?"

"I've heard he got some beef out there with Rich that he's unaware of."

"I haven't heard anything like that. But check this, the other day I ran into him at the store and ya boy is out there wilding. He got a damn candy red Benz and the license plate is encrusted with diamonds on the outside. Not only is he drawing too much attention to himself, but he's also putting us in danger. Especially since everyone knows that you and Money were the reason for his come up."

Murda put his head down. He was truly disappointed in Pop. He saw so much potential in him, yet he was letting everything go slowly down the drain. Murda thought after getting out of the game he would be able to kick back and be a family man, but things never went as planned. Most niggas forgot how to remain humble once the money started to overflow in their pockets, and Pop was no different. Murda still had an open case and here Pop was giving the Feds a reason to investigate more.

Murda took Sharnese's hands into his. Besides Money, she was the only person he could depend on to take care of things. He needed Sharnese to be his eyes and ears on the streets while he was away.

"Listen baby girl, I need you to do me one hell of a favor," Murda said. He hated having to involve her in his street business, but somebody had to do it. "I need you to keep your eyes open on Pop, even if that means following him around town."

"Say no more, you already know I got you," Sharnese replied. Murda's mother Carmen, made it her business to take Sharnese to their shooting range twice a week. She hadn't told Murda nor did she have plans to. Murda wouldn't always be around to protect her. She had to be sure she could defend herself if she ever got caught up in some mess.

No matter how much Murda made her mad, she was ready to ride at all times. In her eyes, a down chick had her man's back even during the worst of times. She couldn't leave Murda when he was down. They had come too far to turn back the hands of time.

"On some real shit, I got a feeling I'm a have to jump back out there and show these niggas how things are supposed to be done. Pop my young boy and all, but I'm not about to let him fuck up the name that I built out here. When me and Money vouched for Pop,

Romario used our loved ones as security. Nese, I can't see anything happen to y'all. I'm already going crazy in here knowing I should be out there protecting you."

Sharnese didn't like the talk of Murda getting back in the game. It had only been a few months since he got out. She knew it didn't matter what she said. If Murda had it on his mind to shut the streets down, then it was no stopping him. She only hoped everything would work out in his favor. Regardless, she would be right by his side.

"I'm not even gonna front, I don't like the sound of it. But I'll support whatever decision you make."

Sharnese took a minute to think about her future. She hoped their marriage wouldn't consist of him always having some type of dealings in the street. She wanted them to be able to raise their family without having to look over her shoulder all the time. Sharnese already had all the answers to the questions she had. When she and Murda first got together, she already knew what she was getting herself into. Being a part of his lifestyle was something she had chosen to engage in. She didn't have to, but for some reason, she felt the need to prove herself to him. She felt the need to show him that she was down for anything when the time came. Being around Murda gave her life thrill and excitement that she hadn't experienced in a long time.

"The only thing I'm asking you in return is to keep it one hundred with me. I'm now your wife and not your girlfriend. Don't have me out here riding for you, while you entertaining these other bitches. I'm telling you, Cortez, one wrong move and I'm filing for divorce," Sharnese said laying the law down to Murda. She loved Murda, but he would not have her out here looking crazy. She was too good of a woman to keep putting up with his everlasting drama. She didn't fault him for the ongoing drama with Journee, however, she did hold him accountable for all the drama they went through with Chanel and Natalie. To this day, it was his fault he was sitting behind bars.

"Come on Nese, I'm a changed man. I was just fucking those hoes. Your love is where it's at."

"You shouldn't have been out looking for no groupie love in the first damn place. If it was sex that you wanted all you had to do was come for me. I mean I know the cookies were on lock, but if you had spoken up, I probably would've reconsidered," Sharnese said. She stopped talking when she noticed that Emily wasn't standing too far from their table, more than likely trying to eavesdrop on their conversation. Sharnese had a trick for her ass though. She knew how to hurt a female's feelings deep without saying anything to them directly.

"So, you want me wearing nothing but my lace black thong and red bottoms when you come home?" Sharnese cut her eyes at Murda and immediately he caught her drift.

"For' sure and make sure you have some candles lit along with my strawberries and whipped cream. You know a nigga tend to get a little freaky from time to time," Murda licked his lips for emphasis. He couldn't wait to get up inside of her and show her how much he missed her.

Emily walked back to the front mad as hell and it showed all over her face. She was setting herself up for failure when it came to playing with Sharnese.

"You know you a trip, right?" Murda said as he stared into Sharnese's eyes. He still saw an innocent little girl when he looked at her. Her soft features would make you think she hadn't done any wrong a day in her life, but Murda knew better since he was the one who had corrupted her soul.

"Who me? What did I do?" Sharnese said in her fake innocent voice. She hadn't forgotten the fact that Emily had been picking on her since she arrived. She didn't mean any harm by anything she was doing. She just wanted to give Emily a friendly reminder, letting her know that Murda was off limits.

"How's my mini-me doing?" Murda said asking about their son. Not being able to see his son on a daily basis fucked with him. He could've had Sharnese bring him with her, but this wasn't a place for children. A riot could break out at any time and there he would've been looking stupid if anything was to happen to him. It was best for him to stay right with Mama Peaches.

"He's doing good. Looking more like you every day. Your mom called right before I left this morning asking if she could keep him for a couple of days. I told her he would be packed and waiting for her this evening. Of course, Mama Peaches put up a fuss about him leaving. I swear she thinks baby Cortez is her son."

Murda chuckled, he knew Mama Peaches could go over the top when she wanted to. But one thing for sure, Carmen was hot enough for her. They were both cut from the same cloth and would pull the straight razor from out of their bras in a New York minute.

"That's what's up. I know she gonna have his ass spoiled as I don't know what. I'll hit her line later just to check on them."

"Boy please, just say you'll be calling to see if Mom Dukes still got it. This isn't her first rodeo, I'm sure she knows what she's doing. I mean she did give birth to you."

Murda sat back and laughed at Sharnese's failed attempt at a joke. "Real funny, now come over here so we can get some pictures taken together. A nigga can't have these horny bastards busting off to the pictures that you sent me."

Sharnese blushed a little. She wasn't expecting Murda to talk about the X-rated pictures she had sent him. "You ought to be proud that you have something another man would want to look at. At least I ain't one of those busted down looking girls. You know the ones you can't tell the difference between who's the man and woman in their relationship."

"Yeah like that over there," Murda nodded his head towards an older couple sitting in the corner, and sure enough, you couldn't tell who was who. The woman had a beard thicker than her man's. Sharnese shook her head. She hoped Murda would tell her if shit got that bad.

Sharnese and Murda posed for several pictures. After finally deciding on which ones they wanted to keep, Sharnese went and got them some snacks from out of the machine. She wasn't even there for two minutes before Emily was walking past her yet again.

"What's the matter, Nese?" Murda asked, seeing Sharnese's sudden mood change. He knew when something was bothering her.

"Nothing. Ya little girlfriend done walked past me for like the hundredth time." Sharnese was doing her best to remain cool. All the other officers were kindly sitting down minding their business while Emily walked around looking for trouble.

"Pay her no mind and focus all your attention on me."

"You have ten minutes remaining in your visit," someone said over the intercom. Murda spent the next few minutes running down everything he needed Sharnese to do; only Sharnese was half listening. She couldn't take her mind off the dirty looks Emily kept giving her.

"I'm a try and find a burner phone from one of these niggas around here so I can call you whenever. I ain't got time to be fighting a nigga over no damn payphone."

"All inmates, please move to the front of the room."

Sharnese gave Murda a long passionate kiss before he was escorted off, by Emily of course. She hated that he had to leave her once again. She only wished he could walk out of those doors with her.

On her way back to the bus, Sharnese ran into Nicety where the two exchanged numbers. Nicety made an appointment to get her hair done at the salon once it was back up and running.

$$$$$$$$$

Murda hated having to take off all his clothes in front of grown ass men. He felt like it was pointless to get searched, being all, you had to do was pay one of the guards to bring in any contraband. Once he got back to his cell, Emily was there waiting for him. *I'm not in the mood for this bitch and her dumb shit,* Murda said to himself. Emily had Sharnese in her feelings over nothing. She had Sharnese thinking that something was going on between them when it wasn't.

"Yo, what the fuck is ya problem?" Murda yelled at Emily. He didn't give a fuck about her being a correctional officer. The level of disrespect she was showing was enough to make Murda catch another open case. The games she was playing were liable to get her fucked up and she didn't even know it. Emily wasn't used to being turned down by any man, but Murda was gonna make sure she became acquainted with it. All the inmates stopped what they were doing to focus in on the drama at hand.

"Wifey must be in her bag," Emily fell out laughing. She was only fucking with Sharnese in hopes of getting what she wanted. All Murda had to do was give her a sample of the dick and she would leave him alone.

"Bitch don't worry about her," Murda said with spit flying out of his mouth. The veins in his neck rose as Emily kept angering him.

"All I got to do is give you the dick and you'll leave me alone?" Murda asked changing up his tone a little.

"Yup, it's just that simple," Emily said as she ran her freshly manicured nails up and down Murda's arms.

"What we waiting for then? Let's get it popping before count time."

Emily couldn't believe that Murda had finally given in. She led Murda into one of the private bathrooms. Emily went to go unbuckle her pants when Murda stopped her.

"No need for all of that right now. I know this might sound crazy, but I can't fuck unless I get some head first." Emily dropped down to her knees prepared to take him in her mouth. She was a pro at what she did, so it wouldn't take her long to give him some quick top. She didn't even get a chance to taste the tip before Murda began urinating all over her hair and uniform. Emily had gotten exactly what she asked for 'a sample of the dick'!

"And I dare you to report this incident and I promise ya kids will be motherless by the sunrise."

Emily said nothing as she sat humiliated on the dirty bathroom floor. Murda had played her and she fell for it. Her days of harassing Murda were up. She had made up her mind that she would be resigning within the next couple of days. Murda made sure that the coast was clear before exiting the bathroom. He had left Emily in there to soak in the hot piss. He had warned her about playing with him, and it just so happened she had to learn the hard way.

Chapter Eighteen

Rich was in the middle of a dice game, giving a bunch of old heads a run for their money. He was already up two grand when one of the old cats tried to sneak a few dollars out the pot.

"It ain't even that serious," Rich said to the man. He had been watching him from out the corner of his eye the entire time. Rich picked up a few bills and made it rain to the ground. He wasn't tripping over a few lousy dollars when he had plenty of them.

"Go head with that shit young blood," the man said brushing Rich off. He wasn't feeling Rich at all. Rich had been talking nothing but cold cash shit about Pop and every nigga that he ran with.

"I'm trying tell y'all nigga, these streets about to be mine real soon. These niggas ain't out here grinding the way I do and it ain't enough money out here for all of us," Rich said rolling the dice. He hit a seven once again, which made everybody quit the game. His mouth was killing the vibe in the room. It was clear to them all that Rich was a straight up snake. He was running his mouth not caring who he was talking around.

"I thought you and that nigga Pop was boys?" asked Slim, the old head that owned the barbershop. Murda and his squad had been nothing but good to him. If it weren't for them, his shop would've shut down a long time ago. Murda had come through for Slim one time when the bank was about to foreclose on his shop. Since then, Slim had nothing but respect for Murda, that and the fact that he was Big Jimmy's son.

"Fuck him and everybody he runs with!" Rich said feeling some type of way. "And y'all can tell him I said it. Pop doesn't know the game when it comes to getting money. He too busy blowing all his shit trying to look fly for these bitches. He ain't nothing but a nigga that bust his gun, and they make plenty of those." The men in the barbershop sat there stunned. They listened to Rich speak so bold about the same niggas that helped him get money.

"You gon have to cut all that bad mouthing Murda and them out or you gonna get the fuck out," Slim said not giving Rich an option. Slim hated the new generation coming up. Half of them didn't know what the word loyalty meant. Some of them even bit the hand that fed them, before they got fed. You could break bread with a nigga, all for them to turn on you in a blink of an eye.

Rich was a thoroughbred nigga. He didn't take shit from anybody. He didn't care how big you were or what set you came from, he had no problem going to work. His hands were official and if he felt he couldn't beat them, then he had no problem busting off his gun. He wasn't about to bitch up no matter how real the situation got.

"What you saying partna?" Rich said invading Slim's personal space. He was so close he could smell Slim's breath.

Rich was popping shit not knowing Slim was an OG. It was surprising to everyone that Slim had allowed him to keep on for this long. Slim had spent ten years of his life in prison and he didn't mind putting his knife in niggas.

"I suggest you go on about ya business before shit gets real." Slim held the blade tight in his hand as he pressed the tip into Rich's stomach. Slim was trying to spare Rich from having to wear a shit bag for the rest of his life.

"Go ahead," Rich said lifting up his shirt, calling Slim's bluff. "Exactly what I thought. Ole scary ass nigga," Rich said as he left out the shop. He let the tension in the shop die down a little before sending a few warning shots through the front window.

Pop, pop, pop!

Rich didn't bother to conceal his identity. He wanted everybody in the shop to know it was him. He didn't need to send anybody to do his dirty work. He ran by himself for a reason. He was tired of niggas taking him for a joke. From here on out, they were either gonna get down or lay down. The streets needed to be cleaned up, and in his eyes, he was the perfect man to do so. Rich could hear the sirens blaring in the background. After letting off a few more shots, he pulled off and jumped onto the nearest exit to his house.

$$\$\$\$\$\$\$\$\$\$$$

"Damn Nese, are you ready yet?" Destiny yelled outside the bathroom door. "I'm not trying to be standing in nobody's long line."

"When do we ever stand in lines? You know damn well we always cut the line and get a few nasty stares thrown our way."

Sharnese came out the bathroom wearing an all-white one shoulder dress with some gold high heels. Her brown skin glistened against the fabric of the dress and everything fit just right. The last thing on Sharnese's mind was to capture the attention of any man, but she had to make sure all eyes were on her. A large bun sat on top of her head with some long Chinese bangs. Looking in the bathroom mirror, she felt like something was missing from her outfit. She reached into her top drawer and pulled out a pair of diamond studs. She had to glance over her outfit one last time before they could leave.

"Enough of all that. Let's go before we are late." Destiny was trying to get there before Money did or else her surprise would be ruined.

When Sharnese and Destiny pulled up to the club, all eyes were on them. They were known to make a distraction everywhere they went. The valet opened up Sharnese's door and helped her out. She went to go hand him the keys but held on to them a little longer when she saw the look in the boy's eyes.

"Please don't mess up my car. I would hate to have to file a lawsuit for any damages, but I will," Sharnese said. She could tell the boy wanted to take her BMW 750 series on a joy ride. As expected, the lines were wrapped all around the block.

"I told you we should've left the house early," Destiny said elbowing Sharnese. Sharnese marched up to the front of the line and immediately the rope was lifted to let them in. Once inside, Destiny and Sharnese made their way to the V.I.P section on the fourth floor. The first and second floors were used for just dancing and drinking, while the third floor served all types of food. A lot of people couldn't afford the cost to get inside the V.I.P lounge, so it was empty compared to the other floors.

"What can I get you ladies?" asked the waitress. She liked dealing with the female customers, the men were always disrespectful. She fought all night to keep niggas from grabbing her ass, trying to steal a quick feel.

"Let me get two bottles of Patron and a bottle of Ciroc Amaretto," Destiny said to the waitress.

"Anything for you miss?"

"Your biggest bottle of Ace of Spades."

"Well damn, I see where all the money is ladies." Sharnese felt like treating herself tonight. It had been months since she had been out of the house. Between taking care of the baby and working in the salon, she hadn't had much time for anything. She was glad Destiny had talked her into coming out.

"We're just some hard-working women over here, that's all," Sharnese replied.

"I feel ya. I'll be glad when I'm finished college so I can get a career. I get so tired of dealing with the dumb shit that I come across."

"Ay, lil' mama with the phat ass," some half-drunk man yelled out.

"That's what I'm talking about right there."

"What's your name?" Destiny asked.

"Nicole."

"What are you majoring in?"

"Paralegal studies," Nicole said.

Destiny jotted down her number on a napkin and placed it in Nicole's hand. "Give me a call once you graduate. I have my own law firm. I might have a spot open soon." Destiny loved seeing black women trying to better themselves. She was always trying to help the next female come up, as long as they didn't bring her any drama.

"Thank you so much," Nicole said with tears in her eyes. She only had a month left before she graduated. She was determined to make a better living.

"You're welcome. Now about those drinks?" Destiny said. Her throat was feeling a little parched.

"I'll be right back with your order."

$$\$\$\$\$\$\$\$\$\$\$$$

"Aye man, you see them two bad ass bitches over there?" Qumaine said to Rich.

"Man, what you talking about? My eyes have been locked on the light skin jawn since they walked in. I've seen her around before, I think she's Murda's bitch," Rich said as he flagged the waiter down. "Yo, send a bottle of Remy over to the table with the two lovely ladies." Nicole turned around to see who Rich was talking about. With the amount of money Destiny and Sharnese had just spent, she knew one bottle of liquor would not impress them.

"Oh them," she smirked. Rich frequented the club every week. He stayed showing his ass trying to lure the next female into his bed. Nicole had almost fallen victim to the bullshit Rich was always spitting. She had deleted his number out of her phone when he had only left her a five-dollar tip. She wasn't trying to keep no man company if he was that cheap.

"Yea them. So, hurry the fuck up!" Rich said getting nasty. Nicole wanted to go upside his head with the bottle sitting on her tray. Niggas like him were why she had to get out of the club. They didn't know how to come out of their mouths. They were always on some disrespectful shit. Nicole walked over and delivered the bottle.

If she stayed in the presence of Rich for too much longer, then she would be out of a job.

"Here you go ladies," Nicole sat the bottle of Remy down on the table. She couldn't wait to hear their response after she told them who the bottle was from.

"Um, we didn't order this," Sharnese said answering for the both of them.

"I know, the man over there sent it over," Nicole said nodding her head in the direction of Rich's table.

"Ain't that Pops' homeboy?" Destiny said to Sharnese.

"You mean use to be Pop's homeboy," Sharnese replied. Rich has been going around town throwing mad shade about the crew. He's been in his feelings ever since Murda and Money handed down the throne." Hearing that changed Destiny's entire mood.

"Send that shit right back. I ain't accepting shit from a nigga that don't fuck with my man or his crew," Destiny fired back.

"Calm down Des. Let's fuck with his head a little bit," said Sharnese. "Nicole please send him a bottle of the most expensive liquor that you have," She hated when niggas tried to show off their money, especially when it was only four digits.

"He could've at least spent a few thousand. Broke ass gonna send a cheap ass bottle of Remy over here," Destiny huffed. She took a shot of Patron to the head. She looked around at everybody in the room. Money and Murda should've been making their entrance any moment now.

$$\$\$\$\$\$\$\$\$\$\$$$

"Man, I knew we should've laid the nigga to rest from the beginning," Murda said. He had heard about the incident at Slim's barbershop, and he was pissed. He kept telling Money to stop sleeping on the young nigga. The hate had been evident in Rich's eyes. They were just trying to figure out why it was so hard for Pop to see it.

"If I'm not mistaken, you were the one who said 'that's a grown man. Let him handle his own problems'," Money said referring to Pop.

"That was before our boy was slipping the way he is now. I've been thinking about coming out of retirement just to handle this bullshit." Money shook his head in agreement. He had been thinking the same thing only he didn't want to make any moves without his right hand.

"Slipping? Man, that nigga done fell way off." Money was trying to drive and empty out the guts of a Swisher at the same time. He needed something to relax his mind. Murda had just been released earlier that day and he wanted to show his boy a good time.

Murda and Money stepped out the truck like celebrities. Paparazzi was steady flashing their cameras. They were trying to get a glance at the two most respected men around town. Women were steady throwing themselves at the two as they tried to make their way inside. The music in the club was on point. Drake's *Legend* was booming from the speakers. The crowd was turnt up, and for once, the drama was at a minimum. Murda didn't fuck with these new school niggas, but he could relate to the song.

When I pull up on a nigga, tell that nigga back, back

I'm too good with these words watch a nigga backtrack

If I die all I know is I'm a muthafuckin legend,

It's too late for my city I'm the youngest nigga reppin, Oh my God, oh my God

If I die I'm a legend, oh my God, oh my God if I die I'm a legend!

A few blunts later, Murda was in his zone and he went to go find Sharnese. He hadn't seen her or Destiny yet so he assumed they were upstairs in the V.I.P section. Murda was on his way up the stairs when he heard somebody calling him by his government name.

"Cortez!" Murda turned around ready to go the hell off on whoever it was.

"The fuck!" Murda didn't even finish his sentence once he saw it was Journee. Murda couldn't stop his eyes from roaming all over her body. The one-piece catsuit she had on clung tightly to her body, which made her ass sit out even more. Journee looked good, but not good enough to make him wanna fuck up what he had at home. He quickly took his eyes off off her. It would be some shit if Sharnese caught him in her face.

"You must like what you see," Journee said as she twirled around, rubbing her hands on her plump ass. *Man, that silicone is gonna be the death of these bitches,* Murda said to himself. Nothing about Journee's ass seemed real. Her cheeks weren't even sitting up even to him.

"Nah, you need to quit fucking with that silicone shit. I like my women natural. Now what is it that you want?" he said getting irritated. The weed mixed along with the alcohol he was drinking had him feeling horny. He was ready to find Sharnese so that he could lay some pipe down. It had been too long since he had been inside of her and he was sick of having to beat his dick every night.

"I would like for you to meet your daughter," Journee said hoping to get on Murda's good side. She really wanted to be back in his life. Too many years had passed by and now she was ready to take what was rightfully hers. If it wasn't for her parents shipping her down south, she would've been raising her daughter in a family environment instead of struggling as a single mother.

"Where are you staying at?" Murda asked. He was ready to get to the bottom of this may be child situation. If Journee's daughter was his, then cool he had no problem taking care of her. But Journee just needed to realize there was no them.

"Downtown at the Hilton. Room 218," Journee said.

"I'll link up with you tomorrow sometime and we'll sit down and talk then." Murda didn't wait to hear a response from Journee. He wasn't trying to hear anything she had to say. She had been gone for over thirteen years and expected Murda to be cool with everything.

$$$$$$$$$$

"Tell me this nigga is really not about to try his hand," Sharnese watched Rich make his way over to their table.

"I just wanted to come over here and personally thank you, ladies, for the bottle," both Sharnese and Destiny nodded their heads. He was sounding like a real gentleman, but it was too bad they had already peeped his bullshit.

"Women of few words. I like that," Rich said smiling hard at Sharnese. The fact that she was Murda's wife made him want her even more. He could tell she was still beautiful underneath all that makeup she had on.

"Nese, I'm going to the restroom. I'll be back shortly," Destiny said excusing herself from the table as she went to go find Money. She couldn't stand to be around Rich for another second. Just him being that close to her made her want to pull out her gun and start shooting.

"No, you can't know my name and no you can't have my number," Sharnese said answering all his questions in one sentence before he could ask. She didn't feel the need to lead him on any longer. She was certain he could see the big rock sitting on her finger. It did shine brightly with the lights in the room.

"Damn it's like that," Rich said. He couldn't lie and say Sharnese was ugly because she wasn't, but he wasn't feeling the stuck-up attitude she carried.

"Yeah, it's like that. I'm married and no I'm not interested in having a side nigga."

"Ya nigga must not be worth shit. I see you out in the club with no man beside you. You must be one of them bitches who don't even give up the ass."

Murda walked in on the last of the conversation. He threw a left hook which landed into the side of Rich's jaw. Rich never saw it coming. The force from Murda's hit sent Rich flying into the table, breaking it into pieces. Murda was enraged. He had just beat a case and here he was in the club fighting, ready to catch another one. The two went at it blow for blow until Rich's face was all bloodied up.

"You must not value ya life talking to my ol lady like that," Murda said still giving Rich the business. He was just about to go in some more when Qumaine sent a blow to the back of his head, knocking him flat on his back. Sharnese snatched the liquor bottle from off the table, she wasn't about to see her man get beat on in front of her. If her man was swinging, then best believe she was by his side swinging with him. Sharnese charged at Rich just as he was getting up from the floor.

"The fuck?" Money said as he entered the room with Destiny. He walked in just in time. Sharnese was wildly swinging her arms at Rich. Before she could throw the bottle in his direction she was snatched up in the air by Money.

"Des, take Sharnese and get out of here." Suddenly, everything happened at once. Money grabbed the chrome Glock tucked in his pants and fired at Rich." At the moment, Qumaine wasn't his biggest concern.

Pop, pop, pop!

Everybody took cover once they heard the shots being fired. Rich and Qumaine fled out the club. They weren't prepared to be in a shootout with Murda and his crew. Money kept on firing until his clip was empty. He was trying his hardest not to hit any innocent victims in the process. He wanted Rich's head blown off. Money was known to be the calmer of the two, but tonight he had shown Rich that when you disrespected one, you disrespected the whole crew. Money was prepared to take control of the situation if Murda decided to prolong it. Just about every nigga that crossed them rarely

got the chance to live and talk about it. With the stunts that Rich
kept pulling, Money felt like it was time to teach Rich a lesson.

"You good fam?" Money asked Murda. He had a few trickles
of blood running down his face, but it was nothing serious, peroxide
could fix it.

"Yea, bro I'm straight. Something must be done about this
nigga," Murda said. Money had just been thinking the same exact
thing.

"It's time to strip Pop of his privileges. It's obvious that he
can't handle what comes with being in charge."

"Speaking of that nigga, is he even here?" Murda asked.

"Now that you said something, I don't recall seeing him
here."

$$$$$$$$$$

Pop was deep inside some thick brown skinned chick named Ember that he'd just met hours earlier. With every stroke he made, she squeezed her pussy muscles tightly around his dick. It wasn't any lovemaking going on, just straight fucking.

"Yes…you better work that dick!" the girl screamed out. Pop smacked her ass a few times as she threw it back. The girl may have had a body like a video goddess, but Pop had no clue that she was only sixteen. Her attitude and body alone had fooled many men into thinking she was grown.

"Stop the bullshit ma, the dick ain't even that good," Pop said as he continued to pound her ass from the back. He loved the way her ass jiggled.

"Yes, oh, yes, right there!" she screamed out in pleasure. Pop was well blessed between the legs compared to some of the others she'd been with. Pop's body was drenched in sweat. She was making him work for his nut.

Bridgette I'esha

"Mmm, this pussy is so fucking good," Pop said as he watched his dick disappear inside and then come out again. Pop felt her pussy getting wetter. He pounded even harder as he felt his nut build up. "Damn," he yelled out as he busted his nut all over her backside. They both laid there breathing hard, out of breath. The smell of sex and funk lingered in the air.

"Yo, where ya bathroom?" he asked, wanting to take a quick shower. The night was still young and he had major moves to make. He needed to make a pop-up visit at his trap houses. The product was missing and the money stayed coming up short. None of his workers were taking him seriously; they kept noticing his fuck ups.

Ember could hear the shower running down in the hallway bathroom. She quietly got up from the bed and searched through Pop's pockets, she counted at least five grand. Not needing to count any further, she snatched up the entire roll and hurried to put her clothes on. She needed to be gone before Pop came out of the bathroom. She didn't know whose house they were in and she wasn't trying to be there when the owners came home. She had lied and told Pop that her aunt had her house sitting while she and her husband were out of town. Ember heard the water shut off, she only had a few minutes before Pop walked out. She was left with no choice but to climb out the window of the three-story home. Luckily for her, it was a fire escape right outside the window. When Pop finally came back into the room, Ember was long gone as well as his money. The loss was nothing to him. *All the petty bitch had to do was ask, I would've given her the entire bankroll,* Pop thought to himself.

Chapter Nineteen

"This is the fifth time this month that money's come up missing! I can't afford to keep taking these fucking losses all because you niggas don't seem to know how to count." Pop was furious as hell. It was about time for him to make a payment to Romario and he didn't even have the money. He was running low on coke so he was left with no choice but to stretch it out a bit. That meant his customers would not be getting the high-quality product that they were used to. It also meant his sales were liable to decline.

"You coming at us when you're the one that's been fucking up!" yelled Zion, one of Pop's younger cousins.

"Little nigga, you better watch how you coming out ya mouth. Don't think you exempt from catching a few bullets just because we're family," Pop said pulling out his gun. He didn't like the fact that someone younger than him was trying to carry him.

"You must be forgetting that we share the same blood in our veins. The same way you'll body a nigga, I will too!" Zion walked into the gun, making sure it was pressed against his temple. He wasn't scared to die and he wasn't about to let a nigga call his bluff.

"I'm just fucking with you," Pop said as he put his gun away. He loved the fact that his blood had heart, which was one of the main reasons Pop had made him overseer of the house.

"Who gonna speak up and tell me where the money is?" Pop said getting back to the matter at hand. Everybody had nonchalant looks on their faces. Nobody gave a fuck about anything Pop was saying. As far as they were concerned, they still worked for Money and Murda, not some nigga that didn't know how to conduct business. "Okay, how about this, nobody gets paid until someone decides to speak up." Pop went to go walk into the kitchen when he heard the house being sprayed with bullets.

"Get down!" Pop shouted from out of the kitchen. He didn't even have time to retrieve his gun before shots were fired again.

POW! POW! POW!

A few seconds later, four men wearing all black had kicked the door in.

"Tie these niggas up," the tall one said. "Remember Rich said to take everything and leave nothing behind."

"Rich," Pop spat out in disgust. He didn't think Rich would take things this far. He and Rich had gotten dough together since they were little boys so he couldn't understand the change of heart.

"Nobody asked you to speak," the man said as he smacked Pop across his face with his gun. Pop spit out a mouth full of blood.

"Man fuck you and that nigga Rich," Pop said. If they were going to kill him then so be it, everybody had to die someday.

"Hmm. You lucky the nigga said to make sure you stayed alive or else I would've put one through ya head for the hell of it."

The men tied everybody up as they searched the house for anything they could take. Everybody looked at Pop with hate in their eyes. He was supposed to be the hitta of the squad and he didn't even try to do those niggas off. Instead, he talked shit the whole time like his life was the only one on the line. The masked men came back down with all the money and coke that was in the house. Zion had never transferred the product to the main location, now they were down to nothing. Zion had already managed to get the rope from off his wrists he was just waiting for the perfect opportunity to grab his gun from underneath the sofa.

"Look at these soft ass niggas still in the same fucking spot," the man smirked. "All this talk around town about his gun game is supposed to be legit, and here he ain't pulled it out yet." The men exited the house the same way they entered. Zion jumped up just in time. He grabbed his gun and ran after the niggas. Everybody followed suit, except Pop, he was thinking about how he would explain the situation to Romario.

Bridgette I'esha

$$$$$$$$$$

Sharnese woke up to Murda's fingers inside of her. She moaned out loud as the sensation felt good to her body. She pushed his hand away as she stood up and took off her bra and panties. She climbed back onto the bed and assumed her favorite position.

"Come lick it," she said as she stared at Murda's large erection through the sheets. Murda spread her ass cheeks apart and licked slowly around her pussy lips, making his way to her clit. "Ohhh, shit!" Sharnese moaned as he sucked on her clit from behind. The vibration of his tongue caused her body to jerk. She had missed the hell out of Murda's tongue game while he was away. Murda pulled his face from out of her ass. He used the back of his hand to wipe Sharnese's juices from his mouth and chin.

"Alright, that's enough," Sharnese said trying to catch her breath.

"Nah lil mama, it ain't no breaks." Murda pinned her legs back as far as they could go, before sliding inside of her wet pussy.

"Did you miss daddy dick?" Murda said as he planted passionate kisses all over her neck. Sharnese had some of the best pussy in the world. He had to pull out a few times to stop himself from nutting so quick. They had been away from each other for too long and he wanted to enjoy every moment of it. "Tell me it's my pussy," Murda said rubbing her clit. It took Sharnese a minute to catch her breath. Murda was putting it down in the bedroom.

"It's all yours Murda," Sharnese said meaning every bit of it. Since she had been with Murda, being with another man had never crossed her mind.

"Damn Nese," Murda said as he felt Sharnese throwing it back. It wasn't long before he was busting all inside of her.

"Damn that was good," Sharnese said as she laid there next to Murda. Ever since he had come home, they had been fucking every chance they got.

"Come take a shower, we got business to handle today," Murda said to Sharnese. It had been a few days since the incident at the club and he had not yet contacted Journee. He was ready to find out once and for all if her daughter was really his. He hadn't even told Sharnese that he ran into Journee.

"How should I dress?" Sharnese asked not knowing what type of business they were handling. She wanted to be prepared just in case something jumped off.

"Like you're the baddest bitch to ever grace the Earth." Sharnese didn't know what he was getting at, but she went along with it. They hopped in the shower together. Sharnese couldn't help but wonder why Murda wasn't filling her in on everything like he normally did. Murda figured the less she knew the better. If he would've told Sharnese they were going to pay Journee a visit, she would've been dressed to go to war.

$$$$$$

"Since when did we start having business meetings in dumps like this?" Sharnese asked. She so used to everything being top of the line, even the Hilton hotel was trash to her.

"Just come on." Murda opened up Sharnese's door and they both rode the elevator to room 218. Murda pressed his ear against the door; he heard nothing but the television playing. He placed his hand on the peephole and knocked a few times.

"Mom, there's somebody at the door," he heard a young girl call out.

Sharnese cut her eyes at Murda. She started to flip out on him right there in the doorway. She couldn't believe that he didn't warn her about who they were meeting. If she would've known it was Journee, she would've dressed in her sweatpants and sneakers. She wasn't trying to be cute when she went to war. Murda mouthed the words 'chill'. He needed for Sharnese to be on her best bullshit. He had never known Sharnese to be insecure over another chick, and he didn't want her to start now. He wanted her to see that she was still the only woman in his world.

"Don't open it. I'm coming," he heard Journee say in the background. Murda backed away from the door just as she opened it."

"Hey Cortez," Journee said in the sexiest voice she could muster up. She had been waiting night and day for Murda to finally come see them. "If I would've known you were coming, I would've put on something a bit sexier." Murda didn't have to respond. Sharnese appeared from the side of the door, making her presence known.

"And you can still catch another ass whipping," Sharnese said pushing past Journee and making herself comfortable on the sofa chair. Murda followed behind his wife and took a seat right beside her.

"What the hell is she doing here? This is about you and our daughter."

"That's where you're wrong. Anything involving my husband has everything to do with me. Now you got one or two choices. Either start explaining why you're finally telling him about his daughter or take this beat down that I don't mind giving you."

"Are you going to say something Cortez?" Journee asked feeling defeated.

"And another thing, you are not his mama and you are damn sure not his wife, you better find another name to call him besides his government name. And the nicknames better not include boo, bae, babe, honey, or sweetie. Get the picture?" Sharnese was not pulling off of Journee; she was laying rules down left and right. If Journee didn't know Sharnese ran the show, then she damn sure knew now.

"Cortez, you not gonna check her?" Journee asked. She wanted so badly for Murda to come to her defense. She could tell Sharnese was Murda's weakness, and with that, she didn't stand a chance.

"No heifer, he's not! But I'm about to check ya chin real soon if you don't pipe it down a notch." Armani being in the room was the only thing keeping Journee from getting her ass whipped. Out of respect for the child, Sharnese tried to remain cordial, but it was about to be forgotten if Journee kept pressing her luck. Murda got up to leave. They had been there for ten minutes already and Journee had yet to introduce them to her daughter.

"Man, I'm out, let's roll Nese."

"Hold up. What is it that you want to know?" Journee asked.

Sharnese took a deep breath and said a quick prayer to the man above. *Lord, please give me the strength. I am trying my hardest not to go in on this chick but she is really trying me,* she said to herself.

"Um, how about everything," Sharnese said being sarcastic. Journee was playing too many games for her liking. Journee sat down in the empty chair as she prepared to tell her story. She grabbed a few tissues from off the nightstand. She always got emotional when she reminisced about her high school days.

"I grew up in a very strict Christian home. Both of my parents were 'holier than thou'. I was dating Cortez in high school and they didn't approve of our relationship since he didn't fit their criteria. Once they discovered I was pregnant, they shipped me down south to live with my aunt. They didn't want the folks at church talking about their image. An unwed, pregnant teenager was not something they were proud about," Journee said with tears in her eyes. She had been forced to raise her child alone. Her daughter had grown up without a father due to her parents being selfish. She had wanted to contact Murda on several occasions only she didn't know how to reach him or so she claimed.

Sharnese clapped her hands together real hard. "Brav fucking O," she said as she continued to clap. Journee deserved an Oscar for the performance she had just put on. To Sharnese, the entire speech sounded rehearsed. She wasn't buying a word that had come out of her mouth. Sharnese turned to face Murda. His facial expression was tight. She couldn't tell if he was mad or just thinking.

"I'm not claiming anybody until I get proof that's she's mine." Murda wasn't taking any chances when it came to claiming kids. He had seen too many of his boys get burned by taking care of children that weren't theirs. He wanted to believe that Journee's story was the truth, but shit wasn't adding up. He just didn't get how she allowed thirteen years to pass before finding her way back to the city. He thought back to the last time he saw her. She showed no signs of being pregnant to him, but then again, they were kids back then. What did he know?

Murda and Journee had been each other's first loves back in high school. Journee had many fooled by the innocent image she displayed. Many thought that she was a good girl who did nothing but go to school and church. The two of them started dating in their freshman year, up until the time she left. Murda had been Journee's first everything. He had explored parts of her body that she didn't know existed. When Journee found herself skipping her period, she tried to convince herself that it was due to stress. Her parents had been pressuring her to leave Murda alone. To them, he just wasn't good enough for their daughter. They had been hearing about his involvement with illegal activity. No matter how much they spoke badly about him, or his upbringing, she never left his side. Instead, she found herself constantly arguing with her parents. She had grown tired of explaining her love for Murda. To her, they would never understand. After missing her period for the second month in a row, she finally went ahead and told her parents, which landed her down in Alabama. She had never gotten a chance to tell Murda that he would be expecting his first child.

"What do you need a DNA test for? She looks exactly like you. What you don't believe me?" Journee screamed.

Sharnese looked at Murda but remained quiet. She wanted to see how things would play out. She knew firsthand how Murda's temper could get out of control.

"Hell, no I don't trust you. This ain't my first rodeo when it comes to bitches trying to pin babies on me. Tell me Journee, what is it you're after. Money?" he said throwing a few dollars her way. To him, Journee was making herself seem like a money hungry hoe. It wouldn't have surprised him if she had heard through the grapevine that he was getting money. You could not walk through the streets of Brooklyn, or New York period, and not know who Murda was. His name rung bells everywhere he went.

"Well, you can meet me at the courthouse tomorrow so we can discuss child support too." That last comment sent Sharnese over the edge. Journee had revealed her true intentions. All she saw in Murda was him being her sponsor. Murda tried to grab Sharnese, but it was too late. Sharnese had flipped the chair over trying to get at Journee. Sharnese had Journee pinned to the ground delivering straight body shots. She wasn't about that hair pulling life.

"Bitch, you just don't quit do you?" Sharnese said between breaths. She had every right to react the way she did, Journee was trying her hardest to sabotage their relationship.

"Sharnese stop. We don't need security busting through those doors." Sharnese and Journee both ignored Murda as they continued on with their battle. Journee continued to scratch Sharnese's face, but Sharnese didn't care, it wasn't anything that a little foundation couldn't cover.

"Bitch you gone learn today that you're no longer the only woman in Cortez's life," Journee spat as she clawed at Sharnese's face some more. "You might as well get used to sharing. I don't give a damn about you wearing his last name. Mark my words, I will too," Journee said confidently.

Sharnese was able to deliver a few more blows before Murda picked her up in the air. "You don't even know who you're fucking with," Sharnese said. "I'll have you come up missing, and that ain't no threat." She swung her legs and her foot landed in Journee's mouth. Sharnese had let Journee get the best of her. She was growing tired of Journee's ignorance. Journee had insisted on being petty, she just didn't know that Sharnese was the queen of petty. Sharnese hulked up a mouth full of spit and spat right in Journee's face.

"When it's all said and done, you will be bowing down to me."

"That's enough Sharnese," Murda said with sternness in his voice. "I said that's enough." Journee was now trying to cut Sharnese with a piece of glass. Murda was beyond disgusted with the way things had turned out. He had two grown women in his presence that were acting like little kids.

Armani sat in the corner unfazed by the drama. She was used to her mother always being in something. Murda stood right in front of Journee with Sharnese over his shoulder as he said a few words.

"If the test results come back to be one hundred percent certain that Armani is mine, the two of you will get along and respect each other. I want... no, my kids *will* grow up knowing each other. And Journee, you will not step foot on our property without my permission," Murda said, finally taking control of the situation.

"Yeah, I hear you," Journee said nonchalantly. She didn't plan on following anything Murda had just said. He was just about to respond when a text message came through on his phone

Money: *Come to the spot ASAP!*

Me: *Everything straight?*

Money: *Hell no, Pop was hit.*

Me: *Say no more*

"Yo Nese, we got to go." Sharnese heard the panic in his voice and followed suit, but not before punching Journee in her face again.

"That's for fucking up my salon." Sharnese was running down the hallway in her six-inch heels trying to catch up with Murda. By the time she reached the elevator, he was already down to the truck. The tires screeched as Murda pulled off leaving the road hot.

$$\$\$\$\$\$\$$$

"You mean to tell me they got you for everything?" Money asked Pop again. He couldn't see Pop being so careless by keeping everything in the house.

"Yea, Zion never did the drop so everything was still here," Pop said trying to throw the blame on Zion, only Money wasn't having it.

"Whose spot is this?"

"Mine," Pop said.

"Who's overtop of these niggas around here?" Money asked.

"Me," Pop said.

"Then, therefore, you are held responsible for anything that happens in your spots. We didn't give you this promotion for you to keep fucking up," Money roared. He was waiting for Murda to come through so they could make their announcement. Business had declined since they put Pop in charge. The fiends were approaching them on the streets trying to find out why the product was so bad. Money was not about to have his name associated with doing bad business. Everybody knew that he and Murda supplied nothing but the best.

"Ain't nobody fucking up over here," Pop said. He was really in his feelings. Lately, everyone around him had been telling him that he wasn't on his game. His workers were turning against him, and now Money was belittling him in front of his crew.

"Let me break shit down to you since it's obvious nothing is registering in that thick head of yours. The entire premises of this house should've been guarded. There should've been shooters across the street as well as upstairs where everything was kept. How many lookouts did you have?"

"None."

"My point exactly. All of this could've been prevented if you took the proper precautions. Now you over there looking stuck on stupid over a simple mistake. A mistake that could've easily cost you your life as well as others." Pop couldn't even argue with Money because he was right. Ever since he had started feeling myself, things had started to go downhill for him.

Money sat down on the couch and sparked a blunt. He let the smoke relax his mind a little, as he waited on Murda.

"What's ya next move?" Money asked Pop.

"Huh."

"Do you have a backup plan? How are you going to get more weight?"

For the last two days, Pop had been thinking about how he would get Romario's money. He barely had ten grand to his name, which was a far cry from the hundred grand that he owed him.

"I was thinking that you and Murda could get him to front y'all some weight and I would pay y'all back over time," Pop said with his head lowered to the floor. Money took another long pull from the blunt. He was sure that the weed was fucking with him. He was not about to get any coke from Romario just to have Pop fuck it up. Pop had shown too many times that he wasn't capable of building an empire. Everything around him was slowing falling apart. Silence penetrated the air for a few minutes as Money allowed the smoke to take over his body.

"You gonna have to ask Murda about that when he gets here."

"What is this a damn meeting?" Pop asked. He knew if Murda was coming out to see what was going on, then some serious shit was about to take place.

Murda pulled into the driveway of the trap house. He parked his Escalade right behind Money's car and walked inside. The smell of weed smacked him in the face as he opened the door. He could tell that Money was puffing on some good shit, but right now he needed his mind clear to take care of business. Murda sat down on the couch right beside Money and got straight to business.

"Plain and simple Pop, we're taking control of things again," Murda said. He didn't want to hear a thing Pop had to say. Business was not being taken care of so a change had to be made. If it meant getting rid of everybody and him and Money putting in all the work, then that's what he planned on doing.

"You can't just come in here, take what's mine, and expect me to be cool with it." Pop jumped out of his chair like he wanted to fight. Murda wasted no time pulling out his tool. He didn't know what type of time Pop was on, but he was bucking at the wrong person. All of the aggression that he was showing should've been taken out on Rich a long time ago. The day the men ran up in the house, Pop had heard the men say with his own ears that Rich had sent them, but he refused to believe it. Rich didn't have a reason to rob him when Pop had turned him onto the connect.

"I can do whatever the fuck I want. Have you forgotten that these streets were mine, to begin with?"

"Fuck you and this weak ass organization." Pop was feeling some type of way. He felt like Murda was trying to play him for a sucka. Over the years, Pop had put in a lot of work for Murda. He had commended Murda for the level of respect that people showed him. It was part of the reason he had wanted to be down with Murda and his crew, to begin with. Murda had shown him the ins and outs of the game, Pop picked up fast, which led to Murda putting him in charge. But somewhere along the way Pop had forgotten to remain humble.

Murda stared at Pop in disbelief. He really liked the little nigga, but he was popping slick out of his mouth when he was the only one to blame. "I understand that you're upset so I'm a let you slide with that slick ass comment."

"Fuck that," Pop spat. "I'm tired of you muthafucka's acting like I can't handle my business out here. I'm in charge and these are my fucking streets."

Murda bit down on his jaw. If Pop had been somebody else he would've been leaking by now. Pop was making it impossible to keep the situation strictly business. It was gonna be a personal vendetta if Pop kept popping shit from out his mouth.

"As far as I'm concerned, there's nothing else we need to discuss. You can let yourself out." Murda wasn't about to let Pop drain him of his energy. Pop just needed to accept the consequences that came along with fucking up.

Chapter Twenty

"Your Honor, this woman is requesting an awfully large amount of money from my client. Let's keep in mind that she kept Mr. Rodríguez in the dark about his child for thirteen years. It's clear that she's after his money," Destiny was pleading her case to the judge. Journee was asking for five thousand dollars a month in child support. And that didn't include health insurance and anything else she could conjure up.

The paternity results had come in just days before stating that Murda was the father of Armani. At first, Murda wasn't sure how he would make up for all the years that had been stolen from him. He had already introduced her to his parents, her grandparents. Carmen fell in love with her on sight. She had always talked about how they needed more females in the family. With Armani being the first granddaughter, Carmen had been spoiling her rotten. Even Big Jimmy was playing his part in giving her the world. He had already started a trust fund for her. He didn't want any of his grandchildren to want for anything. But, it came with stipulations. Armani would be required to have a college certificate or degree before she could touch the money. The same went for Baby Cortez when his time came.

Journee smiled as she thought about the expensive lifestyle she would be living, all at Murda's expense. She had done some research of her own. She knew all about the properties he owned. She wanted a piece of everything.

"Take a five-minute recess," Judge Johnson said.

Destiny knew everything would work out in Murda's favor. She and Judge Johnson had become rather good friends. She owed Destiny a favor for getting her son off a murder conviction. There was no disputing that Destiny was the best at what she did. She didn't like how Journee was trying to carry Murda. She was trying to make it seem like he knew about Armani the entire time and just didn't take care of her.

Sharnese sat on the bench with her hands crossed. She gave Journee a scowl that dared her to say something. Today would be the first time she went to jail for being held in contempt of the court. Sharnese wasn't too thrilled with the fact that Murda now had another child. Nonetheless, she agreed to be supportive of the situation. It wasn't Armani's fault that she had a whore for a mother. She couldn't understand how a woman could be so selfish. Journee hadn't even apologized to either of them for the drama she had put them through. It wasn't like Sharnese had come out of nowhere and destroyed her happy home.

Sharnese walked out into the hallway to get some air. She didn't know how much more she could take being in that courtroom. She stared at the window wishing that the paternity test had read something different. The constant drama between her and Journee had her stressed. She wasn't eating properly and she was barely getting any sleep. She was grateful Mama Peaches was still helping out with the baby or else she would've had a nervous breakdown. Murda placed his arms around Sharnese's waist.

"Everything's gonna work out for the best," he said placing a few kisses on her neck. She wanted to believe the words he said. Lately, she had been finding it hard to believe anything he said. She would ask him how things were going between him and Pop and he would always tell her everything was good. She pretended like she didn't know that Pop had been fired. Murda never kept his business affairs a secret from her, and she didn't see the point in starting now.

Sharnese looked Murda into his eyes, something wasn't right. Her woman's intuition was telling her that he was back to his old ways, but she couldn't prove it. It could've just been her being insecure. She felt like she was fighting for his attention. Everything now revolved around Journee calling about Armani, or so she claimed. Armani was at the age where she could call Murda herself if she needed him. Journee kept bringing up how Armani "supposedly" needed Murda at eleven o'clock at night. Instead of saying anything, she chose to ignore the fact.

"You better hope that it does." Sharnese's frustration was showing and her attitude was at an all-time high.

"What's ya problem?" Sharnese and her attitude were gonna cause Murda to act a fool. Now wasn't the time for her to be acting out. She could save that shit for another time.

"Nothing's wrong with me. Honey, I'm just peachy," the sarcasm was present in her voice. Murda didn't know what was up with her. Lately, she had been moody as hell so he stayed his distance. He figured she needed some space to deal with work. Her clientele at the salon had grown and more people were requesting her services. He thought with the extra money coming in she would've been somewhat happy. Instead, her mood swings were driving him crazy.

"I don't need the smart shit." He opened the door just as Destiny was walking out.

"Hey, the judge is about to read the verdict. Where's Nese?"

"Over there with a fucking attitude for whatever reason." Murda went in and took his seat. He prayed that he didn't have to give

Journee a dime of his money. If she couldn't afford to take care of Armani then she could sign her rights over to him.

"Mrs. Diaz, there are a few things I need to address about your testimony. Earlier you stated that Mr. Rodríguez knew about his daughter and that he failed to fulfill his responsibilities as a father, correct?"

"Yes, Your Honor. That is correct." Journee felt her knees buckle. She was growing nervous while the judge went over everything she said.

"Well according to documents that were presented, that was not the truth. There is no father listed on your daughter's birth certificate and you haven't had a stable job in over five years." Murda was now trying to figure out how she had been able to take care of his daughter with no income. Journee walked around in designer clothes that cost more than an average person's mortgage.

"This man will not be paying you a dime of his money. I suggest that the two of you come to an agreement about how visitation will work. Now if you can't, I'll be more than happy to place the child with the parent who's able to provide a safe environment." Murda wiped the sweat from his forehead. He couldn't give Armani a safe place to rest her head with his lifestyle. He was too deep in the streets to keep track of her all the time and he couldn't risk anything happening to her.

"This case is now closed," Judge Johnson dismissed everyone in the courtroom. She hated when mothers came into her court trying to make the fathers look bad when they played a major role in the way things were.

"Thank you, Destiny," Murda kissed her on the cheek. Once again, she had come through for him. Murda was more than certain he would have to give up a nice piece of change. Now, he had no problem providing for his daughter, but he refused to take care of Journee. Sharnese was his wife and she got up every morning to make her own bread. There wasn't any reason why Journee couldn't do the same.

"Aye babe, I got business to take care of so I'll meet you at the house."

"Okay, I guess I'll stop by the grocery store and grab some stuff for dinner. Will Armani be joining us?"

"Depends on how her mother acts. Make enough for her anyway."

"Alright." They hugged each other before going their separate ways. Sharnese and Destiny chatted up until Journee came busting out the courthouse. She bumped Sharnese with her shoulder. She was pissed that nothing worked out in her favor. As soon as her ten days were up she would be filing papers for child support again. One way or another Murda was going to come out of his pockets.

"Pay her no mind," Destiny told Sharnese. Journee was not worth going to jail for. It was obvious she had nothing going for herself. All she ever did was run her mouth enough so that she could get Sharnese off. Journee was gonna mess around and find herself hurt if she kept on picking with Sharnese.

"Let's get out of here before I mess around and do something crazy." Sharnese pulled her coat closer together. The temperature had dropped compared to a few hours before. She wrapped her scarf tightly around her neck as she walked to her truck. Journee must've thought Sharnese was coming after her with the way she fled out of the parking lot. "Ol scary hoe," Sharnese said to herself. She couldn't stand a female that was all bark and no bite. Destiny pulled up beside her and Sharnese rolled her window down halfway. Destiny would have to talk fast; the cold air was smacking Sharnese dead in her face.

"Make sure you take ya ass home. Don't go following that girl Sharnese." Destiny knew how she could be once you got on her bad side. Sharnese kept to herself. She didn't engage in drama unless it was brought her way.

"I'm not thinking about that girl," she said smiling. "If you don't have any plans you and Money should stop by for dinner. It's been a while since we've all been able to sit down together."

"I'll pick up a bottle of wine. What time should we be there?"

"Six is fine with me."

Sharnese stopped by almost every seafood market within a forty-mile radius searching for all the ingredients on her list for dinner. No matter what time of the year it was she had to have her seafood. Finally done running around, she headed home to prepare dinner and tidy up a bit. She had a missed call and message from the insurance company; they wanted to know if she had turned any evidence over to the police. She would have to lie about the surveillance cameras not working when the incident took place. She still had the tape, but she wanted to handle things her way. She didn't trust the videotape being in anyone's hands but her own. She didn't want the police to be able to link her to Journee in case something happened her.

$$$$$$

Destiny had just laid the kids down for a nap when there was a knock at the door. She checked on the kids one last time before opening the door. Instantly, she was met with a blow to the face that sent her down to the floor.

"Ahh!" Destiny screamed as she tried to fight off her attackers.

"Grab that bitch so we can get the fuck out of here," The unfamiliar woman yelled.

"I'm trying to, she's strong as fuck!" Destiny's heart was beating rapidly. Not only was she scared for her life, but her children's as well. Destiny had no clue who the male and female in front of her was. Destiny kicked and screamed some more hoping someone would hear her cries for help.

"Shut her the fuck up before someone hears her!" Destiny cringed in pain when a steel-toe boot landed on her face. Blood from the open wound ran down the sides of her checks. The cries from baby London caused her attackers to stop dead in their tracks.

"Nobody said anything about a baby. The fuck we supposed to do now?"

"Take the baby as collateral."

"Please don't hurt my baby!" Destiny screamed. She kicked and clawed at the man, but it was to no avail.

"Bitch shut the fuck up!" The unknown man grabbed the baby from out the room while the unknown female-led Destiny out the door.

"Make any dumb ass move and I swear to God this will be the last time you see your daughter."

Destiny remained quiet. She felt like a complete failure. Her job as a mother was to protect her children and she failed. A little sense of hope came over her when she realized that didn't find Little Sincere. She was guessing he hid somewhere once he heard all the commotion. As smart as he was, she was praying he picked up the phone and called Money. A bag was placed over her head and her body was thrown into the trunk of the car. Destiny couldn't remember falling asleep. She wasn't sure if she was awake or dreaming when she saw two faces she hadn't seen in years. Queenie and Syrius Ketant. Her parents and powerful leaders of the Haitian Cartel.

To Be Continued....

CPSIA information can be obtained
at www.ICGtesting.com
Printed in the USA
LVOW13s2316040618
579618LV00010B/223/P